THE USE OF REGRET

THE USE OF REGRET

a novel

by

Greggory Moore

Several portions of this novel have appeared previously. See the back of
this book for a list of these and related acknowledgements.

Library of Congress Cataloging-in-Publication Data
Moore, Greggory, 1968–who knows when?
The use of regret / by Greggory Moore

10 9 8 7 6 5 4 3 *

(I had no idea what these numbers signify, but I always see them in other
books, looking all slick, so I figured, Why not? Then I looked it up: it's
how you tell what printing of a book this is. But what does that mean when
you're self-publishing in the electronic age? Yeah, I don't know, either. I'm
calling this sort of the third printing, because I've made two batches more or
less minor but totally stylish improvements since it first came out.)

ISBN 1-448-68671-7
EAN-13: 978-1-448-68671-1

Cover design by shea M gauer

THE USE OF REGRET

We the People, in Order to form a more perfect Union

We Came In

For example, we can revolve around a character, me, you, anyone can play, speak for them or let them speak for themselves, sing for their supper, try, let them try. Choose a story among numberless stories, tell it however you choose, then another and another again. These are life as I imagine it, collected, recollected, the world as it was and could not have been, as it appears now and will come to be, uneclipsed, that life, mine (and yours). This is me putting back together what was never all apart, the way, the story, let me tell you, how I wish, this story, let me tell you.

**

You Are Here

[1] We Came In [2] **You Are Here** [3] Americana 101 (Early 21st Century) [4] I Dream of Bicycles [5] A Weekend, Early [6] Color Me World [7] In a Bakery [8] Museum Piece [9] Out [10] Place Names and Places A [11] Was It Kant [12] Rain [13] Momentum [14] Apparently Following [15] Embellishment (a poem by Todd Balazic, found in a magazine, poorly understood and used for future inspiration) [16] Room [17] Another City of Light (on the Wane) [18] Taj Mahal [19] What Use Regret? [20] Here Out There [21] In Orange, a City in the Modern Age [22] Every Ear a Snowflake [23] Undermusic [24] An Awakening [25] Eddie and Eugene Kim [26] Faith (Maybe It's True) [27] Seven, Nine, Eleven, Twenty-Seven [28] Rain [29] The News [30] Forever [31] Bliss (Once During Lovemaking) [32] Ephemera [33] Every Snowflake a Snowflake [34] In King County, Washington [35] Some Total [36] Dog Girl [37] Brother Paul, What a Dick [38] It Turned Out that Reality Was Overrated [39] Can't Help But See [40] Teeth and Other Things [41] Comeback [42] Selected Philosophical Terms [43] What the Might-Have-Been Meesus Said about Self-Representation [44] Husband, Father Killed by Drunk Driver [45] The Sick and the Dying [46] Call Him Jim [47] Rain [48] The No [49] Embellishment (a poem reconsidered) [50] Life That Never Is [51] Place Names and Places B [52] A Few Remains [53] Art Appreciation 101 (Early 21st Century) [54] Once During Lovemaking (Another Time, Another Place) [55] Nature vs. Nurture [56] Greetings from Amsterdam [57] My Struggle, It's Nothing [58] Jack Valenti Is Near Death (One of Our Jokes) ® [59] Remission [60] She Told Me; I Did Not Tell Her [61] Faith (I'm Afraid It's Not) [62] Room II (the Concurrently-Running Sequel) [63] Three of the Happiest Days of Our Lives [64] The Amsterdam Gods [65] The Use of Regret [66] Can Be, Can You [67] Face [68] The World's Longest, Most Philosophical, Stupidest Greeting Card [69] Bridge View, Part 1 [70] Place Names and Places C [71] I Was Thinking of You [72] Ceci n'est pas une pipe [73] How They Say It [74] The Last Man on Earth [75] Dinner with Him and Her [76] An Old Dog Anew [77] Bridge View, Part 2 [78] Seawall [79] Gravid [80] Favorite U.S. Pastimes 101 (Early 21st Century) [81] Blood Is Thicker [82] What She Might Be Like [83] Taxicab Horror Stories, No. 80,911 [84] Remember, Forget [85] After a Lifetime of Healthy Living [86] U.S. History 101 (Early 21st Century) [87] The Travel [88] The Very First [89] Blindness, Close [90] 20 Most Popular First Names (US) [91] Lament for an Unpredictable Coat [92] It's Strange to Try [93] I Can Only Paraphrase [94] Another Time, Another Place [95] Animals Killed by Airplane Refuse [96] People and Places as Words [97] Mailboxes, Et Cetera [98] I Should Have Written [99] Sleep Baby Sleep [√-1] √-1 [   ]   [1(00)] Isn't This Where

Americana 101 (Early 21st Century)

For the sake of further convenience, a matching series of hanging signs labels the components of the outdoor mall: KB Beauty Supply, Gilmour Nutrition, The Right Mail Box, Good Sport Water Sports, Kimi-Kai's Koffee, Masonry and More. A malformed little man sits cross-legged on the sidewalk, greets many of the passersby. "Hi there. How are you? You're a pretty lady." Flies hover so steadily in the shade it seems they are suspended on wires. An American flag at one end of the parking lot is moved by a breeze that does not seem to reach another two farther down. "How are you? Have a great day. God bless you." A willowy girl, beautiful but for terrible acne, laughs along with two male friends, wanting them to want her, looking into their eyes, laughing, wanting. A toddler spins in place, almost falls, spins again. Three skateboarders push themselves by, one hoisting his board up and stomping it down as if hopping over a wall perceivable only to himself. A car alarm sounds, is virtually ignored. "I'm not rude. I'm a great man."

I Dream of Bicycles

I dream of bicycles, of riding bicycles a hundred feet high. I'm never conscious of the absurdity, I'm just riding, pedaling from a great height, looking down on the intersections I pass through, the cars I fearfully somehow manage to avoid. I strain and wobble, knowing a crash or fall could happen any time. I negotiate a turn, a traffic jam, with dumb luck avoid a pile-up. I bunny-hop the two wheels onto an overpass, wrenching the towering machine up to the eight lanes of perpendicular concrete, then letting it drop back down while somehow staying upright, aloft, somehow continuing on my journey to I don't know where, I never know where.

A Weekend, Early

Saturday: One week earlier the television had serenaded the small boy with a story about the beginning of how the United States is Constituted. Today it sang that every person he could know, every place that he could go, any thing that he could show are nouns, including: *you, word, name, I, school, house, clock, state, home, street, dog, brother, island, summer, friend, snow, neighborhood.*[1]

Sunday: The adults talked and smoked and tended to the barbecue. Hotdog aroma hovered within the wooden-fenced yard. The children swam and floated on inflatable animals and rings. Lean Larry, a quiet paterfamilias, one-sixteenth Choctaw and a

---

[1] *History*, a noun with a trickier tangibility, was not included, though its subtending presence animated the entire composition.

trainer by trade, held his son on a muscular knee.

"Tell me I'm a noun, Daddy, and bounce me!"

"You're a marshmallow. You're a marshmallow" and bounced up and down. "You're a marshmallow." He thought of his chubby child stuck through with a fork "You're a marshmallow" held over a fire "You're a" roasting and burning "marshmallow" flesh curling and melting "You're a" fat liquefying "marshmallow" charred, dead, having suffered. *I don't want to be here,* he thought, *I don't want to be here.* His son laughed. The children splashed and screamed. The hotdogs were being eaten.

Color Me World

I envision a world colored by my attention. I regard something for a moment and it goes a certain shade; I concentrate or focus and its newly acquired tincture deepens, glows, cycles itself along a pre-established spectrum. Particular hues could indicate specific cathexes: I look at you a hundred times and you're platinum, a thousand and you're fluorescent teal; a painting moves me deeply and it's forever gilded with a pinkish vermeil blush. The colors could be real, the world bearing the stamp of my mind for all to view: He glanced here often without thinking; he loved you more than life itself; he never caught a glimpse. Or they could be only self-reflecting prisms: Look at all the pretty colors of my private, private world.

In a Bakery

There was not a moment in which, in some way, on some level, Carol was not with him. When separated from her, he, Robert Stanley Singer III, the luckiest man in the world, a man who had written his own story, might think of the texture and sheen of her auburn hair or the unmistakable change in her eyes that occurred every time she smiled sincerely. There had been moments since the first time he had kissed her seven years ago when he would suffer a mild convulsion of realized desire simply with the random remembrance of her supple fingers resting against his chest, or of her lips gently pressing on the wanting of his mouth. She had been forever implanted into his experience. Even during the long stretches while his conscious mind was occupied with other thought, there existed something on a deeper and all-pervading level (be it the subconscious or the soul) that kept her with him and brought a succor and sufferance to whatever trial or mundanity he might happen to encounter.

It was on this level she was in Southern California, in their adopted hometown, at the Rue Linda L., reading the *Register*, sipping from a Styrofoam cupful of coffee, eating a pink-frosted donut while the dawn sunlight seeped through the windowpane.

He closed his eyes midsentence and took in an aroma just as the airliner on which she was returning hurtled its final thousands of feet south into Tower 1. He sipped his coffee and returned to the story, touched with a molecular enjoyment, the barest awareness of freshly baked bread.

Museum Piece

They had put up a sort of plaque (they, someone, who exactly being not entirely clear prima facie, though educated guesses could be made), saying:

This exhibit is like any exhibit: it's meant to show you something that was salient for someone else (and may be for someone else again). It has a place in a context, a context we could never fully give you, however we might try. But you are here, reading these words. And that's something.

This exhibit never changes, but please come back to be with us again, because there is always more to see.

Out

I had planned on going out. Just go out, I said to myself, you want to go out. I felt like going out when I said it, I wanted to be out right then I think, or liked the idea of being out, not being alone, out in public, with people. But it took so much less effort to stay in, stay there, be alone, not having to suffer the conscious-ness of being seen, of having my appearance perceived, my actions interpreted. But I'd planned on going out, Just go out, I said. I felt good, felt well, wanted to be out, the idea of being out, felt like not being alone (even though alone is so much easier in so many ways).

Shower, shave, choose and put on clothes. Should I pee before I go? What do I need to bring? My coat? Where are my keys? Do I have enough cash? It's a bother. My energy seemed to fluctuate, my will, the impetus to keep progressing toward an end, just go out. And I'm going to be seen. I could just stay in, watch TV, smoke a joint, so easy, I could just wait until the weekend and go out with friends. But the idea of being out, Just go out, I said.

I locked the door, I'm out, on my way out. I feel okay, up to going out, this is good. It's nice out, I've got the right coat, I've got my wallet, okay. I walked to the corner, rounded it, passed by a planter of flowers in front of an apartment complex. The smell flashed a memory. "Terry," I said without thinking, not to her in apostrophe but in recognition, the Spanish *conocer*, like That's Terry, that smell.

I reached the shopping center's parking lot, heading for a bar at the far end. I looked out beyond the giant American flag and the lights to the black above them, the black in between the necks of the overhanging streetlamps. I thought about feeling the darkness around me if the light were extinguished, a blackout or the death of all technology. The lights were falsehood but viscerally I believed. A sudden lack of illumination while I was out and exposed would feel colder, my desired lie failing to shield me from the truth of darkness and a crescent moon.

The lights stayed on, comfortably dishonest, and I reached the bar. Do I want to go in, I asked myself, feeling less resolved, not wanting to be seen but wanting not to be alone, desiring the idea of being out, whose reality is more problematic, it's so much simpler to be alone. Just go out, I said, I want to be out. Just go in, you're already out. I went in.

The jukebox was playing the Pixies, somebody was singing along: *'I like Lou Reed,' she said, sticking her tongue in my ear.* I was in. I'm in, I'm out. It was more crowded than I had hoped, I was unsure where I could sit. If I have to stand I'm leaving, too conspicuous, I'll feel too self-conscious just standing here. A couple of empty stools were at the end of the bar, perfect, I sat. I looked to the bartender, he was too busy to notice me. I waited, he did not notice, I felt conspicuous. I moved to the middle of the bar, squeezed my way in between two patrons, one looking at me as if I were intruding. I leaned forward, trying to establish eye contact with the bartender (busy and not noticing me). Finally he leaned my way, two fingers resting on a red cushioned ledge on his side of the bar top. "May I have a 7 and 7, please?" He nodded (without looking at me) and went to mix the drink. One of the patrons next to me laughed with monstrous, disgusting exaggeration and swayed back, bumping me into the other, who glared at me again. My drink came, I paid for it, the tip too big but I felt an unspoken pressure not to ask for change. I extricated myself from the bar and made to return to my original spot, but both stools were occupied, there was nowhere else to sit. I sipped my drink, it was not very good. I'm out, I said. The jukebox was playing: *Caribou, caribouoooo.* I didn't want my drink anymore, didn't want to have paid for it, didn't want to stand there out, exposed, the problematic reality, the reality not the idea. I looked at the people, so many of them, none alone. I knew it would be like this, what was I thinking? I swallowed from my bad drink, I looked around, not wanting to make eye contact. There was nowhere to sit. I wished for a power outage, wished for invisibility, wished for an escape. I was out, this is being out, remember for the next time. But you won't, I said, you'll want to be out, the idea of being out. And you'll go, just go out, you will.

The jukebox was playing, the rest of the bar had joined in: *We're chuh-ained, we're chuh-ai-eened. . . .*

Place Names and Places A

Cincinnati/Northern Kentucky International Airport, CVG (Covington). From Cincinnati: Drive south on I-71 or I-75 across the Ohio River. Take Exit 185 and follow the I-275 circle freeway west to Exit 4 (State Route 212). Follow the signs to airport terminals and parking facilities. From the west: Follow I-74 to the I-275 circle freeway. Follow I-275 south, then east to Exit 4 (State Route 212). Follow the signs to airport terminals and parking facilities. From the south: Take I-71 or I-75 north and go west on I-275 to Exit 4 (State Route 212). Follow the signs to the airport terminals and parking facilities. 6 miles from Florence, 12 from Covington, 13 from Cincinnati, 15 from Lawrenceburg, 17 from Newport, 35 from Kings Island, 37 from Hamilton, 60 from Dayton, 72 from Lexington, 77 from Frankfort, 98 from Louisville, 125 from Indianapolis, 130 from Columbus, 262 from Cleveland.

Was It Kant

Was it Kant who said that language creates the world for each? Someone did, and however much it's true it explains the gap between us, the unbridgeable gap from here to there, from I can see to you out there. Kant or whoever was talking about culture, the unchangeable difference between one and another because of the windows through which we view the world. The world for each differs, which explains why I can't explain the why or what of anything to you out there, because I think and it's not language, not the words but something else I can't impart if it's true that you and Kant and whoever else other unreachably out there thinks like me, not just like me but generally thinks not the words but something else, each a language of our own, untranslatable, incommunicable. If this non-shared language that is everything in here, even when I think the words . . . There are words but it's not the words if that something private language which is everything, if language shapes the world that confines each of us to his own world, her own world, and me in my own world created, never shared

I try, I can't but I try, I talk, I say something, words, but how-ever well I speak them they're never the not-the-words I wish to say. Even as they leave my mouth I wonder why I try, and from here I hear them not be not-the-words, I feel them leaving, disowned by me, not being what I want you out there to have, not giving what I want to give of me; they're not me. I recognize myself in here and however much I don't understand, I know that what I emit is something else, is caused by me but isn't what I want to cause, the effect is never really right out there, you take something in that is not me, why try when it can't be right, it can't, another of so many things, so many goddamned things, bad enough but worse when damned from the start, before the start, eternally irreconcilably damned. Why create something that can only fail, why try to save whatever's damned, why give life to something dead, why reanimate the inanimate, why bring it back, why not leave it buried, why dig it up and try and fail to explain the remains, why not let it rest in peace? Another thing I can't explain especially when I know the remains are not the thing but me, they're me, which is both the last thing I want to talk about and the first thing I want to impart, at last, at first, to try, to fail and be left with me by me, an inadequate version at that, not to say I'm adequate but at least if I could represent myself, if I could create a me that would be something other but this

Rain

"Well, thanks for the ride," he said, patting him on the right shoulder.

"No problemo."

"Looks like rain."

"Oh, I love it when it rains," she said, turning halfway around to regard him with an enthusiastic smile. "I wish it would rain more."

He gathered his coat as he contemplated the storm clouds.

"Not me."

Momentum

Terry was sitting on a plastic bench meant to look like a cut-open tree trunk. Her new sports bra was causing her discomfort, and from time to time she would absentmindedly pluck at it through her T-shirt. She was lost in thought (lost to us, surely) and staring straight ahead, and we can only approximate her internal monologue, taking poetic license as necessary &c.:

The pond is flat, fluid glass. A gentle, steady wave pattern is moving right to left, swooping arcs. I'm moving towards Saturn not far above its rings. I'm looking at the big sky, I'm looking at the big sky. Dusk is coming, and bugs crash into the surface, invisible insects like raindrops at the beginning of a gentle storm. I should still be jogging, I was going to do that hill at least two more times, why am I so tired lately, maybe I'm just depressed, it's only been two weeks since we, since he. Night's coming and I'm not dressed for it, I just want to sit here, to stay, to be still and take in the slow, grand movement of the world, the air, the ripples, day becoming night, a rocky mass of land and water revolving around the nearest star. Momentum is everything, and I feel none. The night is coming, it can't be stopped. If I stay I'll be cold. So I'll be cold. I'll live.

Apparently Following

They looked like they were following each other, one after another, always in pairs, companion pinpricks from a local constellation come to say hello. Soon the nearest ("highest" in my image of the two twinkling specks of white) would appear to be slowing, then make its way to my left on final approach to the airport, the other eventually circling behind. I imagined it would be possible to plot the schedule of arrivals the way Galileo and Tycho Brahe charted movement in the heavens. But in my case there seemed no point in making the effort. I just sat there night after night, watching them fly, inferring something about the truth, a truth, perhaps.

Ones that cruised closer seemed less patterned and never partnered, their blinking multicolor and shadowy adumbrations passing much faster across my field of vision, seeming less stately, less graceful. Helicopters occasionally buzzed overhead, outward into the darkness above the city grid. They would touch me indirectly by shaking the air, vibrating the room, a momentary visitation, an avatar of a rotary creature, an eidolon here, gone. That was my only company that first semester in grad school, that and a lineage of French and German philosophy. I figured I better buy a cat.

[Wait and see.]

Embellishment (by Todd Balazic, a poem found in a magazine,
  poorly understood and used for future inspiration)

Had we actually been out in the rain
it might have gone differently.
But we were on the sidewalk,
under an awning.

"I don't want it to end this way," she said.
She looked at me, her eyes like a second voice
saying, "I don't want it to end this way."
I was looking out at the street where

the rain fell, anticipating how powerful
it would feel to deny her. "Nevertheless,"
I said, "this is the way it ends."
I even touched her cheek.

Walking home I remembered a blue glass.
It was a favorite of hers, a gift
from her sister, and I remembered how
after dropping it I itched with distress,

those blue fragments looking up
from the white kitchen tile, and she
laughing, saying not to worry,
not to worry.

Room

You're sitting in a chair in a white room. At various times in various places messages flash in a language seemingly familiar to you. You read: $X + Y = Z$. What can you say about X, Y, Z? You read: *I love you.* Are you loved? You read: *You're in a white room.* You stand up. You read: *You stood up! Simple or composite?* You sit down. You read: *Doggone gene plan plant mind that's y'all mouse mice meesus.* You kiss the chair. You extend a hand. You read: *It looks like rain.* You gouge out your eyes. You feel what you believe to be blood on your hands, your face. You wonder whether the messages still flash. You feel pain.

Another City of Light (on the Wane)

I'm watching this guy shaking. He's just sitting on this stool at a slot machine, his eyes closed, arms folded around each other almost affectionately, shaking. Every now and then he has a little spasm, a minor seizure, but he does not seem to notice. He looks to be in half-conscious thought, perhaps sleeping or dreaming.

I'm walking in the direction of this really tall cocktail waitress. She's moving down a row of 25¢ video poker machines, taking drink orders. She has those enormous thighs that a lot of tall women have. I wonder how many sizes larger her tuxedo top must be than the standard issue. She's maybe 6' 4", 180 pounds. I wonder about how much hairspray she used to get her hair to stay that still, and if she thinks about how big she is when she looks in the mirror. She does not see me as I squeeze by her.

I'm waiting for an elevator. No one else is there until a petite, dark-haired woman walks into the foyer. Her heels click to a standstill, but she does not look up until the chime of an elevator's arrival. The doors thrust themselves open. I walk in and turn around; the woman does not move. I hear another chime, and her heels clack in that direction as the doors that slide in front of me cut her out of view.

I'm looking at this maid. She's pushing a steel cart in my direction, looking down at the blankets and sheets stacked neatly on top, or at the hallway floor, or at nothing in particular. Her nametag says GISELE. I pass by, seemingly unnoticed.

I walk into my room, into its dark stillness. The light comes on with the flick of a switch, but the room is just as still. I sit on the bed and look at the face of the digital clock: a flashing 12:00. I pick up the TV remote and push POWER, but the screen remains dark. I push the button repeatedly, pointing at various angles: nothing. I give up, my arm falls. I move to the window and look, but whatever view there might have been is eclipsed by the hotel across the way. There are no visible lights in any of its rooms, only the obsidian blackness of unilluminated glass at night.

Taj Mahal

1. An integrated complex of structures, it took thousands of persons to compose one man's vision. He built it after she was dead, so it was an ultimately empty gesture, empty because unable to convey his love to its target. Empty like saying "I hope" after

the matter is decided: *I hope she died painlessly*; *I hope she really knew how much I love her.* Hope if you must, but the die is cast. The hope is inappropriate, chronologically at the very least, unless you can undo time or make some things come around again. You hope his project served another purpose, for his sake, something beyond simple indulgence. Someone says he said the following of this work: *Should guilty seek asylum here, / Like one pardoned, he becomes free from sin. / Should a sinner make his way to this mansion, / All his past sins are to be washed away.*

2. Grammy® Award-winning blues performer active from the 1960s until early in the 21st century. Sample lyric: "Further on down the road, baby, you'll accompany me / That's what I'm hopin' for."

3. An ornate hotel/casino in Atlantic City, NJ. The work of a self-centered man with grandiose plans.

What Use Regret?

I couldn't really see her; the sun was in my eyes.

"And so that's it? That's it?" she continued with that appalled surprise that had marked her end of the entire conversation. "Seven years, just like that? Over this. Over *nothing*. This is fuck-ing ridiculous."

"Nevertheless," I said, knowing she would hear my intended

ellipsis, knowing it would annoy her.

"Oh, you're such a character, ha ha." She popped me on the left side of my chest with the palm of her right hand. "What are you doing?"

"What do you want me to tell you, Terry?"

She waited for me to say something more; I remained silent.

"Jesus," she laughed, wiping her eyes. "This is you? I didn't know this was you."

Me: "No one ever knows or loves another."

"Oh yes. Do that. Quote to me. That's *delightful*. You're so fucking clever."

"What can I tell you? I just don't . . . Look, this has made me see that . . ."

She shook her head gently. "Shut up."

I glance her way every few syllables as I compose my words: "Hey, I know it's bad timing, that you've been funky, in a funk, whatever. But hearing it now is better than . . . Hey, look, you know, so what, right? I'm the bad guy. Does that make you feel better? Fine, you know?" I looked at her, considered touching her, looked. "We'll stay friends. Hey, give it some time. It'll work out. It'll be fine. I'm sure this is for the best. And you're young, you're attractive. You'll have no problem . . ."

She wasn't angry now. She let me gaze at her face, open as

ever, let me see her hurt, her pain, what I'd done, letting me have the victory if that's what I was after. She turned, stopped, waited, walked away.

Here Out There

I can see from here out there to you in that world that is other than here, here not being a place, a physical locus but this, the personal private me, the first-person narrative, the as far as I can tell, which does not extend out there yet somehow includes you, the out there other you. As far as I can tell I said, but maybe there is something more, I'd like to think, it's a nice thought. But I can see from here to there, that other world, not me as far as I can tell, at least that, and that's the point, the feeling me not you, that separation, that's the first thing I'm aware of, the first memory. I was 3 years old, mother other, not a thought, not these words but something I knew, I looked at her, "Smile" she said, an eye behind a camera, *camera* a thing that records an image, an image a thing but not the thing it represents, the words not the words but something other I could see from here, I knew the difference.

Flash and it's a memory I see out there, 4 now and mother and I walking by a building with windows black, no light, I could *1-2-3*, 3 stories, black windows, 3 blind mice, a vertical row slowly progressing in my sight, 3 blind mice slow racing in a dead heat with the earth turning, turning, and she holding my hand. Did I know where we were going? I do not now. Her hand wet sweaty uncomfortable to hold, my hand squirmed, I squirmed it, sliding, clammy, disgusting, other, foul, did not pull away, not quite. I wanted her to release, to release me, release, the other, to stop forcing itself, forcing, on me. I could have pulled away but didn't.

The world out there, the other, it does not change like I the me in here. The other flows in static clumps of cause and effect. The sky changes color for a reason, a book stays a book, but I am selfsame and erratic, searching for the permanent province of me, an island of Iland, the everchanging neverchanging, the imaginary I, the real i, the two eyes, the third eye, a flowing point of view. I watch and interact, but in here I'm somewhere else, quantum in a classical world.

We are not together so what can I tell you, how can I explain: a snapshot, a postcard? There is nothing like that I can give, there's no postal service to or from these parts, not yet as far as I can tell, not yet. I'd like to think that one day, somehow, a nice thought, but since not yet and we are not together, how can what I tell you explain how I can snapshot flash and record an image memory, the picture other than the thing, both mine and other too, but was it at the snapshot flash, as the bulblight lasted, just as it died away, did I die too, a me that was a point of view, looking through the viewfinder, 3 days before they told me, I looked and pushed a button, trying to capture what I saw, what I see, what was here, there. Was it the moment? No, I knew, I snapped shot anyway, I thought it worth the time. Flash there and now the image, two dimensions, flat, dead, color fading.

A picture's worth etc. but how much does that say when we talk about us? There is an other others may perceive as me, that they might label me ("him"), but that's not much, not me, and I oughta know, I've been here a long time, longer than the stars and you and any other, mother, father—don't bother, brother. The picture was of my sister this time, here it is, not her. She was 3. I knew I was 15 of course, at least as well as I knew she was 3, I thought *She's 3*, this creature I had seen newborn, not the words but a thought in the moment, at least that, because there it is now when I think of it, and here it is, *She's 3*, and I know by addition that I was 15: 12 years older than she; ergo, 15. I take it on faith because of the steady predictable nature of you out there, the other that now includes the past, the me then not here inclusive, not this temporal locus, this first-person phenomenon of me/now. (Ugh.) I'm sure it's right, I was 15, but that is not part of what I remember of that snapshot, the me then in that moment looking through the viewfinder was conscious of her age, *She's 3*, while I took the picture, not the words but something in the flash, something that was in here. She was 3 and smiling, loved me (loved, even then?) and I remembered her first day, *Smile* I said, she giggled, that smile, that not the words. I loved her laughed and took the picture. The bulblight dies. Now we are somewhere else.

Everything dies in fact, the natural way of things they say. I die, the me of then is not me now so he's dead, something remains but not that me, it's not here, it's other, it's dead. My sister in the Polaroids, she was gone before they developed, before they even slid out of the camera, that moment fled, that smile faded, she cried, she smiled again and laughed, she turned 4 and 5 and 6, then 7, and had she turned 8 that girl would be dead now too, the she then, the she at 8, so it's not so different now in that sense and I shouldn't feel so bad. Everything dies, I'll die too, I die every moment but one day we'll transcend even that, I'll be other than this, I'd like to think the nice thought that at least something

Why those moments now, why not when my mother told me *Perry, I've got bad news*, she said it just like that: *I've got bad news*. I remember now, it's there in here somewhere, accessible, *I've got bad news*, it was so odd, *I've got bad news*, but it's not there now like *Smile* and her giggle at 3, that picture, the awareness of her being 3, not the words, not a consciousness, but here it is as part of that snapshot memory, she was 3, I knew it, I cannot tell you in just what sense, you have to be here to be it, I can't explain.

Casablanca I thought when my mother said *I've got bad news*. I'd known our goose was sick of course, she had been for a long time and we knew she would die, everybody dies, but there was no reason to expect it then. She had been sick for a while, they didn't know but there was no reason to expect, and it was a semester abroad. My mom (Polish-Hungarian, had never traveled outside the U.S.) said *Go*, I went to Amsterdam and fell in love for the first time with words and an outside her and called weekly from the café on the corner. I had made love and smoked a joint and had straight Bs and was so happy to call home and speak with my littlest love. For some reason I imagined she'd be feeling well and we'd have a lovely chat, not knowing my relation to love (word and not-the-word) was about to change forever. Mother answered, "Hello, Mom" I gushed. The day was beautiful, I was looking at the canal, a black inner tube bobbing up and down on water that smelled like no water I had ever smelled, of feldgrau and concrete and beauty, "Hi" she said, there was something awkward but I was stoned and happy, "It's been a lovely day in Amsterdam." She didn't say anything. "How are you, Mom? You there?" "Perry" she said, "I've got bad news." *Casablanca* I thought, my favorite film then. I knew *She'll never see it*, but it was neither words nor explicit knowledge, just an unconscious guess, educated and as it happened right. Had it been wrong the thought would have been the same, the moment, *Casablanca*, but as it happened *Casablanca* is connected to *I've got bad news* because she died that morning just after they all woke up. *Tell Perry I love him*, Mother could barely get that out. I was stoned, *Thank God I'm stoned* I thought.

I came back for the funeral, not that I really cared, I didn't buy in to symbols, I knew it was other than caring, that mourning did not require public consensus. But I came back and stayed because I thought I should I don't know what, confront it, that to stay in Amsterdam and smoke and study and live a life I loved, the happiest then up until then, that it would be denial. Maybe it helped my parents, my being there, but that was not why I returned. I should have stayed. I was in love and alive, and I shut down and didn't let her in because I knew she couldn't be here. She was other, she could not know, no routes leading in, it was the same as always but it was a different me then, I don't know why now and here I am now thinking of her, the past, so much past, so much that might have been different.

"Here you go" she susurrated, passing the stack of syllabi with both hands as if imparting a secret, a sacred offering with a smile. I passed them along without looking, keeping eye contact. "Hi," I extended a hand, we shook, we touched, "I'm Perry." "I'm Asya" she said, "Asya" I asked, "Asya" answered Asya, "Let me spell it for you." Asya laughed, *Asya*, "What" I asked, Asya answered, "I think I was trying to be sexy or something" she laughed, *Asya*, she laughed, I was in love, I think, would it be love now?

She whose name I never speak, whose label I use, *sister*, but whose name I have not applied to her since the day she was interred, which was a cold day, overcast, the weather exactly like Amsterdam's when I had left. "You can't beat the weather in Southern C-A, hey?" my Uncle Pat from Boston said that day. "Why are you here" I wanted to ask, "We hardly know you," *we* meaning my sister and I, but I just said "Yeah." "How was Amsterdam?" "I wish I had a joint right now" I said, knowing this would put him off. I'd had quite a bit to drink, "Thank God I'm drunk" I muttered to myself, "Thank God I'm drunk" I said a little louder, "Thank God I'm drunk." Others could hear that I was talking to myself but could not make out the words, "Thank God I'm drunk." I turned my face in the direction of the fewest people and let some weeping slip, "Thank God I'm drunk" I said. They put her in the ground with pomp and circumstance that would have meant little to a 7-year-old and meant nothing to me nor to the person I imagined she would have become, a person I would never meet, a person with a name I wouldn't hesitate to utter. "Ashes to ashes" said someone working for the funeral home,

"Funk to funky" I sang and sniggered, "We know Major Tom's a junkie," extended family and friends looked at me askance, the orator pretended he did not hear me hitting an all-time low.

"How was Amsterdam" I was asked repeatedly at the wake, "How was Amsterdam?" "I loved it" I said, knowing I should have stayed, not the words but knowing, already feeling the futility, the uselessness of watching the descending casket, the flowers and dirt thrown on top, the catered spread, turkey and ham on little pre-cut rolls, the mayonnaise and mustard clinging gently to white plastic serving knives, macaroni and oil salad. I continued to drink. I loved my sister, I had come back from Amsterdam, I was talking to myself, I got very ill and spent most of the wake vomiting in the bathroom, *Thank God I'm drunk* I thought. I was still drunk when I emerged, everyone was gone, I finally had something to eat, the house was almost dark, my parents had gone for a walk. I sat on the new couch in the living room, the one they had gotten during my absence, a fold-out for the nurse. They're right, I thought stupidly, it doesn't feel like a fold-out. I wonder whether they'll sell it now, I should have said something to the nurse, should've thanked her, should've gotten beyond "Hi, nice to meet you." I was drunk, thank God, but she was there for my sister, she took care of her. It was too hard on my parents, too much, and me, I missed her death, missed her, I should have been here, I should have known somehow, I should have loved her enough to stay no matter what. Is that it: I didn't love her enough? I knew that it wasn't; I cried with the guilt and self-hatred that it was. *I should have been here, I should have been here, I should have stayed with her.*

In Orange, a City in the Modern Age

Shakespeare never heard
cars
on a freeway
in the distance
the gentle whirr
of high-speed rubber
on a concrete path
eight lanes wide
winding east
winding west
the constant thrush
of displaced air

Every Ear a Snowflake

It was the period in his life when her brother was spending all of his money and time on his car. "See, I've got it set up so that you're always in the sweet spot."

"What's the sweet spot?"

He smiled at the opportunity to educate his sister. "The sweet spot is when the sound from all around—left and right if you've just got stereo, but from both left and right and front and back if you've got quadraphonics going—when it hits you at just exactly the same time. When each moment of what comes out of the speakers hits you just as when it left, you're in the sweet spot. I've got it set up so that you're always in the sweet spot. Check it out."

"How does it know exactly where you are?" she wondered.

"Huh?" he would have answered.

"How does it target you with perfect specificity? I mean, how does it know, say, how high your head is, or at what angle your head is turned? How does it know when you shift your position? And is it the sweet spot just for the driver? Come to think of it, each ear is unique, is at least a slightly different shape from every other ear in history—even from its counterpart on the other side of your head; and so the 'sweet spot' would be dependent on whose ears are involved, if we're talking about getting it *exactly* right. You're saying you've set it up to account for all this? And by the way, do you realize you're getting excited about *a sound system in a car*?"

She said none of it. He was her big brother, and she loved him. "Let me hear it," she responded to his goofy smile. "Ooo, let's put on *The Wall*! That would be totally cool!"

Undermusic

1. I think it's too intricate for its own good. But what the hell

am I gonna do about it? I mean, no plan that would work for this would be simple enough to pull off, would it? I don't know. All I do know is that I've got to get the hell out of here. But I don't even know whether I've thought it through properly. Ah, it's just bullshit, anyway. It's just words. It's not worth mentioning.

2. A man walks into a bar. He orders a bad drink of some sort (it doesn't matter why), but he can't think of anything snappy to say. So he sits on a stool at the bar and listens to the regulars sing. He's got his drink but not his seat (it doesn't matter why), but he can't think of anything snappy to say, anything that's worth mentioning.

3. So few people play chords the right way, the long, slow, drawn-out chords truly availing themselves of all vibrational possibility, the spatial chords pointing to something before the notes, something beneath the actual music. It's not the technical skill then, but the ear, the feel. They don't paint the picture in full, they don't fill in the emptiness, but they function on a quiet, subverted level. One, two, three . . . slow, and incomplete (in a way). Simple (on the surface), but reaching into . . . what? I don't know. I could show you if things were different, I think. But I can't explain it. I don't have the language. I was just mentioning.

[But listen.]

An Awakening

According to his blue-glowing digital clock, he awoke at precisely 4 a.m., believing he had been awakened. What could have awakened me, he thought, saying it to himself like that, *awakened me* and not *woke me up*. He squinted at the clock to make out the numbers: 4:00 AM. Hm, why did I awaken?

He opened the refrigerator and peered inside. It's not hunger, he thought, closing the door. But something awakened me. "Hmph," he said out loud, "strange."

He stood in the middle of the living room, looking about. Well, he thought, something must have happened. Is something about to happen? He walked over to the telephone, half-expecting it to ring; it remained silent. His cat entered the room, looking at him, then the ceiling. Absently he followed the cat's gaze, though she had already lost her interest and turned away. Later on, I will know that, whatever it was, it happened at exactly 4 a.m., he thought. And that it awakened me.

Eddie and Eugene Kim

They moved in across the street when I was 8 and became my friends immediately. It was a suburban housing tract replete with children, and they fell right into our milieu. This included show-and-tell, and they gave me my first glimpse of uncircumcised penis, something I did not even know existed, this other, foreign form of being.

One day at recess a group of us were together on the grass next to the blacktop. Someone had made a joke about my duck-like waddle, and everyone was laughing. Eugene was nearest to me, lying at my feet, literally rolling with laughter, and I stomped once on his abdomen, enraged, embarrassed, lashing out, wanting it to stop. I had no thoughts of damaging him; in some sense I was unaware of the possibility. He writhed in pain but was not seriously injured. A teacher escorted us to the office, and together Eugene and I waited for our parents. He wasn't angry; I didn't know what I felt. He was not allowed to play with me anymore. I understood why, and I ruminated on what I had done, how I had caused him pain while lacking the specific desire to do so. It was my first explicit sensation of remorse, of the reality that my actions could have consequences outside of me, outside of my intentions, consequences that could run contrary to my wants. I had apologized to Eugene, and I apologized again at school. I went to see his parents and expressed how sorry I was. They relented, and I treasured the Kims until they moved to Los Angeles a few years later. We made efforts to stay in touch, had two sleepovers (one in S.F., one in L.A., having forgotten all about the mystery of otherness), but in prepubescence the absence of day-to-day involvement can be fatal to friendship, and by the end of middle school we had drifted, became lost to each other.

It's Christmas Eve of my senior year in high school, and there's a knock at the front door. I open it to see a Korean boy roughly my age. "Hi," he says. Then, with a smile: "You don't recognize me." I look, then feel the answer before I give it. Eddie smiles again; I am benumbed. I invite him in. He exchanges greetings with my parents, my mother displaying the overexuberant falsity she habitually took on to convince herself she felt more than she really did, that she felt what she thought she ought to feel. Seeing that we are in the middle of opening presents, he declines to stay, saying they were back in town seeing relatives (they had moved to Honolulu two years earlier) and he had just wanted to stop by, say hello, wish me a Merry Christmas. The visit is five minutes. I watch him walk to his car, wave, drive away. The sadness is novel, unrecognized, like the Spanish *no conocer*. I mount the stairs (thirteen, steep), turn left (beige carpeting), my right hand pushes the door handle (black-stained metal), open, close, walk to the bed (unmade), turn, sit. I sit for a minute, two, I'm not sure how long, then begin to cry. I do not understand his coming here, I do not understand my reaction. I cry and begin to recognize what is paining me: I am cut off from Eddie Kim, Eugene, from everyone, inevitably. I could never have predicted his finding me again, can never fathom the depths of his reasoning, the impetus, his seeking me out on this or any night, his experience, that separate internal world. I can never do better than infer his emotional state, guess at it, and I sit and cry, knowing that he cannot feel me. He might be happy or sad this Christmas—I could not know for sure from here. At that moment he might be listening to the radio of his relatives' station wagon, he might have come hoping for an impossibly magical reconnection, he might be having exactly the same reaction I am having—I could not know. At that moment were he bleeding to death from a ripped femoral artery, there was no way I could feel it. I would never know unless the next day I happened to see a news story about a SoCal Christmas tragedy, a Korean boy from Hawaii out for a drive who bled to death after his car was hit head-on by a drunk driver who suffered only minor injuries and was taken into custody at the scene. "Oh my God, that's Eddie Kim," my mother would moan. "He was just here." Her face would contract, the folds of her neck flushing crimson. The tears would flow. Slowly she would burst into wails, building: "Oh, oh!"

Faith (Maybe It's True)

You make this gesture like this, she said, her forearms tight to her chest, clenched fists upturned almost in supplication, whenever you talk about feeling closed off, focus turned inward, and I know what you mean. And maybe it's true, maybe that's the way it really is: we're all closed off and isolated, there's no world behind the scene or whatever you say when you quote Sartre, I don't know. But I have to believe otherwise. I have to live as if I'm really in contact with you and my family, my friends, strangers, everyone and everything. I have to believe that, because otherwise what is living? Maybe you do understand existence better than I do, maybe it's really like that, maybe no one ever knows or loves another, but I don't care. I'm here with you, right now, we're together, this is living. That's all that matters, that's all that matters to me.

Seven, Nine, Eleven, Twenty-Seven

There were two of them, one and one, an I and I, identical in many ways but really quite distinct, and they were felled, first one, then the other, on an ordinary day, with people coming and going, making love and eating cake and reading the news and smoking a joint and smelling bread and murdering prostitutes and hearing rain and naming our children and looking at maps and regretting so very much. People die all the time, all the time, are always dying, but this seemed different, particularly tragic, a symbol in blood, something we would never forget. Never is a long time, but we only live so long, so long, so long.

Rain

She bounded out of bed and directly to the window.

"Look at it, look at it!"

She grinned as if she were finally experiencing something long imagined but never directly known.

"Look at it," she whispered to herself, "look at it."

The News

"Hi, Terry. Please, have a seat."

"Thank you."

"Can I get you something to drink?"

"No, I'm fine, thanks."

"Okay. Terry, I need you to prepare yourself, because I'm afraid I've got bad news."

"Oh. Oh."

"You have what's called T-cell prolymphocytic leukemia. It's unusual for a woman of your age and ethnicity to be stricken with this, but our tests are conclusive."

"Leukemia?"

"I'm afraid so."

"Leukemia."

"Are you alright, Terry?"

"Leukemia. My God. How, how bad . . . aren't there different . . . What did you say it, what is it?"

"It's called T-cell prolymphocytic leukemia. T-PLL for short."

"Is it . . . how, mmph. How serious is it?"

"I'm going to be blunt with you, Terry: there are several different types of leukemia, and this is one of the worst."

"Am I going to die?"

"There are things we can try, some drug and radiation therapies. But this is a pretty rare form of leukemia, and we haven't had a lot of success in treating it."

"Oh my God, I can't . . . believe it."

"Can I get you anything, Terry?"

"No, I'm okay. 'I'm okay.' Ha. I feel sort of numb, you know? Uncomfortably numb, you might say. That's a joke "

"Terry, we don't need to talk about this any further right now. I suggest you go home and get some rest. We'll make an appointment for a few days from now, once you've had a chance to digest this, and we can discuss our options then. Do you have anyone at home?"

"We, I just . . . I'm living with my parents right now. My

boyfriend and I just . . . How long?"

"I'm sorry?"

"How long? How long do I have to live? It sounds so cliché."

"Well, Terry, there's no way we can say. We don't even know what the best course of action is at this point."

"But probably . . . how long?"

"Terry, I really can't—"

"Please. Anything is better than not knowing. I know you can't say for sure. I'll sign . . . papers . . . indemnify you. . . ."

"Terry, first, you've got to keep this in your head: you're not necessarily going to die.

"Everything dies. The natural way of things."

"Sorry?"

"Nothing."

"As I said, T-PLL is rare, and we just don't have a lot to go on."

"But."

"But, for most people at this stage, from what we know, somewhere between six months to a year."

"Six months. That's not even until Christmas."

"Terry, please . . ."

"No, I know. It's okay. I just . . . It's okay. I'm fine. Really.

I'm afraid, but it's okay."

Forever

I remember and oh that time you made that face like and laughed and said and the way you looked that book your hands and sitting by pretending and oh remember when we went and heard the way the trees and forest smelled and after how we cried and saw and said that we would never and what was it that man did while we were walking by and oh then that time you tried to give and standing on the seawall looking at the ocean staring at the sunlight deflecting off the swells "I wish I had a coat" you said and I gazed at iridescent you and told you I'll remember this forever.

Bliss (Once During Lovemaking)

She was naked, grunting in ecstasy at the man she adored. He watched her beneath him, writhing, saw the cellulite bulging and bouncing lightly on the outside of her right thigh. Despite his own paunchiness, he felt disgust, a disgust of which she was completely ignorant.

I don't want to be here, he thought. *I don't love you anymore.*

"I love you" he said.

This isn't real. I can't trust you. I don't love you anymore.

"I love you" he said.

Ephemera

Hidden within a Utah canyon is the GRANITE MOUNTAIN *RECORDS VAULT, the largest single repository on Earth of information about the dead.* Records, photographs, and documentation of all sorts regarding over two billion people are collected there; and with each passing day its contents are expanded. Most of the records (especially those of individuals who died without living relatives) are never viewed.

Now and again the United States launches an unmanned rocket that deposits a camera-equipped rover on MARS, *a lifeless world, the fourth planet out from the sun in our solar system. If ever humans live on planets other than Earth, the first undoubtedly will be Mars.* It rolls around in a rather limited and uneventful way and snaps a few hundred photos of that barren landscape. In general, people are enthralled with the whole business (seemingly forgetting previous probes that sent back similar images), but I become consumed with the little cars only as their power fades. Completely isolated from the Earth, the inert machines exist as much then—and now—as they had when millions of people were following their daily movements. I think about them sitting forgotten underneath those salmon skies, accumulating in number, one at a time.

F. SCOTT FITZGERALD (1896–1940). Novelist and short story writer credited with chronicling the "Jazz Age" and considered one of the greatest writers of the 20th century. He quickly rose to international prominence in 1920 with the publication of his first novel, This Side of Paradise, *but his fame was short-lived. His greatest literary triumph was* The Great Gatsby *(1925), but the book received only mixed reviews and did not sell well. His other novels include* Tender Is the Night *(1934) and the unfinished* The Last Tycoon *(1941). At the time of his death, most of his works were out of print, his celebrity long forgotten.*

I was meandering home from making two deposits in Utah and ended up on Highway 120. At 4 a.m. I pulled over to rest. I pissed over a ledge, then noticed the enormity of the heavens. I had never been privy to such an unobscured view. I saw not dozens of pinpricks of light but clumps and clouds and clusters of stars, shading and spackling the whole of the sky. And yet, for all the suns visible there, and for all the innumerable, inscrutable points so legion they appeared as luminescent haze, all that I saw was only a small part of *THE MILKY WAY, an ordinary spiral galaxy (ca. 200,000,000 suns) in an indistinct region of space in a universe the size of which we cannot fully measure.* But we do know that, with the expansion of the cosmos, we are becoming more and more alone, moving farther away from everything.

Every Snowflake a Snowflake

One night, long before she was born, I lay on the carpet floor of a mountain cabin, watching them fall, luminescent, feet in diameter, falling, silent. Fractals and iterations were readily apparent in the radial shapes gracefully descending through the blackness (though I was decades away from first hearing such terms: *fractals, iterations, descending through the void*). Each floated down past the eaves and into view, falling in staggered formations at a constant rate. For hours I stared at the procession of never-repeating designs, unable fully to grasp the detail of any one of them before it gently abandoned itself to the accreting pall of white, whose softness bore an inverse relation to the extirpation it visited upon the feathery crystals dying there. "The snow kills them" I said to my father, who did not notice and went on talking with the other adults. I was crushed that the stuff of life and death, of variety and homogeneity, all was one, and finally I ran to the door and out into the snow, overcome with the need to redress such unjust desolation. But there was only coldness and wetness, and I could not see the snowflakes now, and my father's thick hands gripped my upper arms and hoisted me back inside. He asked me why, but I could only weep, hysterical as I watched them continue to fall and die and realized they had never been alive, had only briefly taken these forms that were destined to pass away, to break and lie and melt and never again exist as they had for a drifting flicker in space and time.

In King County, Washington

The Judge has asked me to state what I did in my own words that makes me guilty of these crimes. This is my statement:

I killed the forty-eight (48) women listed in the State's Second Amended Information.

In most cases, when I murdered these women, I did not know their names. Most of the time, I killed them the first time I met them and I do not have a good memory for their faces. I killed so many women I have a hard time keeping them straight.

I have reviewed information and discovery about each of the murders with my attorneys, and I am positive that I killed each one of the women charged in the Second Amended Information. I killed them all in King County. I killed most of them in my house near Military Road, and I killed a lot of them in my truck, not far from where I picked them up. I killed some of them outside. I remember leaving each woman's body in the place where she was found.

I have discussed with my attorneys the "common scheme or

plan" aggravating circumstance charged in all these murders. I agree that each of the murders I committed was part of a "common scheme or plan." The plan was: I wanted to kill as many women I thought were prostitutes as I possibly could.

I picked prostitutes as my victims because I hate most prostitutes and I did not want to pay them for sex. I also picked prostitutes as victims because they were easy to pick up without being noticed. I knew they would not be reported missing right away, and might never be reported missing. I picked prostitutes because I thought I could kill as many of them as I wanted without getting caught.

Another part of my plan was where I put the bodies of these women. Most of the time I took the women's jewelry and their clothes to get rid of any evidence and make them harder to identify. I placed most of the bodies in groups which I call "clusters." I did this because I wanted to keep track of all the women I killed. I liked to drive by the "clusters" around the county and think about the women I placed there. I usually used a landmark to remember a "cluster" and the women I placed there. Sometimes I killed and dumped a woman, intending to start a new "cluster," and never returned because I thought I might get caught putting more women there.

My statements as to each count are as follows:

Count I (1): In King County, Washington, sometime between July 8, 1982 through July 15, 1982, with premeditated intent to cause her death, I strangled Wendy Lee Coffield to death. I picked her up, planning to kill her. After killing her, I placed her body in the Green River.

Count II (2): In King County, Washington, sometime between July 25, 1982 through August 12, 1982, with premeditated intent to cause her death, I strangled Debra Bonner to death. I picked her up, planning to kill her. After killing her, I placed her body in the Green River.

Count III (3): In King County, Washington, sometime between August 1, 1982 through August 15, 1982, with premeditated intent to cause her death, I strangled Marcia Chapman to death. I picked her up, planning to kill her. After killing her, I placed her body in the Green River.

[...]

Count VII (7): In King County, Washington, sometime between May 2, 1983 through May 8, 1983, with premeditated intent to cause her death, I strangled Carol Christensen to death. I picked her up, planning to kill her. After killing her, I placed her body in a wooded area in Maple Valley.

Count VIII (8): In King County, Washington, on or about July 17, 1982, with premeditated intent to cause her death, I strangled Gisele A. Lovvorn to death. I picked her up, planning to kill her. After killing her, I left her body near the southern boundary of Sea-Tac Airport.

Count IX (9): In King County, Washington, on or about August 29, 1982, with premeditated intent to cause her death, I strangled Terry R. Milligan to death. I picked her up, planning to kill her. After killing her, I left her body just off Star Lake Road.

[...]

Count XIX (19): In King County, Washington, on or about September 26, 1982, with premeditated intent to cause her death, I strangled Linda Rule to death. I picked her up, planning to kill her. After killing her, I left her body near Northwest Hospital.

Count XX (20): In King County, Washington, on or about October 8, 1982, with premeditated intent to cause her death, I strangled Denise D. Bush to death. I picked her up, planning to kill her. After killing her, I left her body just off a dirt road in the neighborhood of Riverton. I later transported some of her remains to a place just off the Bull Mountain Road, near Tigard, Oregon. I left the remains there, with the remains of Shirley Sherrill. I did this in order to throw off police investigators so that I could continue killing prostitutes.

Count XXI (21): In King County, Washington, sometime between October 20, 1982 through April 9, 1984, with premeditated intent to cause her death, I strangled Shirley M. Sherrill to death. I picked her up, planning to kill her. After killing her, I left her body just off the Auburn-Black Diamond Road. Later I transported her remains to a place just off the Bull Mountain Road, near Tigard, Oregon. I left her remains there, with the remains of Denise Bush. I did this in order to throw off police investigators so that I could continue killing prostitutes.

[...]

Count XXVI (26): In King County, Washington, on or about April 17, 1983, with premeditated intent to cause her death, I strangled Kimi-Kai Pistor to death. I picked her up, planning to kill her. After killing her, I left her body near Mountain View Cemetery.

Count XXVII (27): In King County, Washington, sometime between December 1, 1982 through December 31, 1985, with premeditated intent to cause her death, I strangled an unidentified woman referred to as Jane Doe "B16" to death. I picked her up, planning to kill her. After killing her, I left her body near Mountain View Cemetery.

Count XXVIII (28): In King County, Washington, sometime between December 1, 1982 through December 31, 1985, with premeditated intent to cause her death, I strangled an unidentified woman referred to as Jane Doe "B17" to death. I picked her up, planning to kill her. After killing her, I left her body near Mountain View Cemetery.

[...]

Count XLI (41): In King County, Washington, on or about October 30, 1983, with premeditated intent to cause her death, I strangled Denise L. Plager to death. I picked her up, planning to kill her. After killing her, I left her body at Exit 38, just off I-90.

Count XLII (42): In King County, Washington, on or about November 1, 1983, with premeditated intent to cause her death, I strangled Kim L. Nelson to death. I picked her up, planning to kill her. After killing her, I left her body at Exit 38, just off I-90.

[...]

Count XLV (45): In King County, Washington, on or about March 13, 1984, with premeditated intent to cause her death, I strangled Cindy A. Smith to death. I picked her up, planning to kill her. After killing her, I left her near Green River Community College just off Highway 18.

Count XLVI (46): In King County, Washington, on or about October 17, 1986, with premeditated intent to cause her death, I strangled Patricia M. Barczak to death. I picked her up, planning to kill her. After killing her, I left her body near Seattle International Raceway, just off Highway 18.

Count XLVII (47): In King County, Washington, sometime

between August 4, 1998 through August 6, 1998, with premeditated intent to cause her death, I strangled Patricia Yellowrobe to death. I picked her up, planning to kill her. After killing her, I left her body just off Des Moines Way South in South Park.

Count XLVIII (48): In King County, Washington, sometime between July 23, 1971 through August 31, 1993, with premeditated intent to cause her death, I strangled an unidentified woman referred to as Jane Doe "B20" to death. I picked her up, planning to kill her. After killing her, I left her body just off Kent-Des Moines Road.

Some Total

The numbers seem almost meaningless, there are so many of them, not even counting the imaginary. Known quantities in one context are entirely absent in another, even as the numbers retain their shape and apparent familiarity. Sequences are constructed ad hoc at cross-purposes. Applications multiply and divide, join and part company, label and obscure. One eye for seeing, two eyes for seeing—it never ends. But here and there an order is discerned, orders, multiple, clusters, a concordance, and for a single moment there is wholeness, all falls into place, encompassed and dissolving so that even all no longer applies.

There is just   . And then you move in order, into sequence, present, past, and you count and calculate and think about what is missing, and the enormity is upon you, the infinite that renders your efforts moot, where you find yourself while conscious of your loss. You are here, you are here—a mantra of both real and unrealizable presence, the paradoxical wish to both lose and locate while drifting in-between, reaching but not touching, unable to rest finally on either shore, unable, and yet . . .

Dog Girl

I didn't like what the treatments did to her, the operations, the morphine. Let her die, I used to think, to want to say, just let her die, I love her, let her die, am I the only one who loves her. But I had missed my chance. Just before she was born we got a dog. "It's Jerry, after this year's #1 draft pick or Gary, after Big Hands Johnson" said my dad, a trainer with the 49ers. "Jerry" my mom chose immediately. "Jerry Montana. What do you think, Perry" he asked, "Jerry Montana," knowing I could not have been more thrilled, having been programmed to love the Niners, educated about their lore, knowing not just that the Catch had a capital C but also that the commonplace American names Dave Wilcox and Billy Wilson had special meaning. "Jerry—that's your name" I cooed, "Jerry Montana. Yes that's right, that's you. You look like that, don'tcha? Yes oh yes, Jerry Montana Gregson." I loved him with that automatic love a child feels for his first dog. But by the time she was born it was clear he was ill, on a downslide, and when the vet said amputating a leg was no guarantee the cancer would be stopped, I wanted to say no, wanted to talk about not diminishing his quality of life, wanted to differentiate for my parents living well and living, wanted to explain that life did not have inherent worth, that it could be bad, that if they loved him they would not even chance that he might wake up from the anesthesia and lament the missing limb, suffer through those first unfamiliar steps. Maybe if they could guarantee that he wouldn't mind, or more importantly that the pain he had begun to feel would be no more, that his vivacity would return. I wanted to say it, but I didn't have the words. The cancer had spread, he suffered for 2 more months with just 3 legs, and before being as they said put to sleep she was born. I wondered whether they would make the same unloving mistake with her if something similar came to pass, never imagining it really would, never even fearing it until they told me she was sick, when they told me, when they told me.

3 nights later, after the image flash and bulblight death, I looked in on her, so small, so doomed. I wanted to kill her, to snuff out the chance that this little girl would suffer, knowing otherwise she might be left to languish, forced to live. I should

have killed Jerry, should have taken him to a park and held him lying on the grass, held him, hugged him, told him 1 last time how much I loved him, utterances he could never really understand, then shot him with a gun from my dad's collection, maybe the .38, the 9mm semi-automatic. I should have been a killer. I looked down on her, I touched her forehead then jerked my hand away, not wanting to risk disturbing her sleep just because I yearned to be as close to her as I could, have that bond of touch, feel her breathe. It would take only a moment if I struck her hard enough, if I picked up something heavy. I looked around: the table lamp, its metal base, I could unplug it, loop the cord around my hand, remove the lampshade in case it would make noise as I lifted it above my head carefully. Would I hear a small creak or the vibration of the harp, the whisper jangle of the filament as I brought it down full force, careful with my aim. Would it crush her skull, split open her head or simply bounce against it, I would hit her several times in rapid succession before it felt like anything, before the horror of snuffing out my little pixie registered, I could do it, I can do it, almost the words. I was sweating, an alkaline taste in my mouth, shaking, dizzy, a little hard to breathe, enervated, failing, I felt about to collapse, I began to cry, stopping my mouth and nose with my empty hands, *I love you, I love you.* I turned and left the room as quietly as I could, heard the door brush twice against the shag carpeting, whoosh, whoosh, knowing that was as close as I would ever come to saving her no matter how bad it got.

Brother Paul, What a Dick

"Do you think tension can kill you?" Jim asked seriously, pressing at his sternum as he sat on the bed. "Jesus."

"Sure," Paul sang out enthusiastically. "High blood pressure, hypertension—that shit can lead to a heart attack or stroke. No joke. Narrowing of the arteries, I think it is, contraction from tension over time, some fucking thing."

"No, but I mean, like, immediately, instantaneously. Like, 'Geez, I'm tense'—then, you know, *boom*: stroke, heart attack, you keel over—whatever. Just from tension." He palpated a spot on his chest, then another, then another as he took a deep breath. "Like if you're not tense most of the time, but one day something happens, it tenses you out so bad that your body completely freaks out, stops your heart, seizes you up."

Paul's gaze was trained on the mirror image of his pink bowtie and his tugging fingers. "And there's nothing wrong physically, like brain damage or anything?"

"Right, no."

Paul took Jim's face in his hands playfully, like he might do to a puppy. "But you're tense in general, boopie, my little tense boopster."

"I am not," Jim pouted.

Paul returned to the mirror, pulling the crotch of his slacks so as to free his scrotum from being pinched by his new briefs. "Sure you are. You just don't realize it."

"Whatever. But can you die like that?"

"Boopie boop, if somebody seizes up from stress enough to die, believe me, they've been no stranger to stress."

"Do I act stressed-out?" Jim queried.

"Well, not so much—for a guy with a stick up his ass."

"You really think I am?"

"Yeah, boopie," (singing) "boopie, my looooooove." Paul watched Jim press on his chest with his other hand, then with both. "Nice tits, baby?"

"It's definitely tension," Jim said tightly. "Uh. I'm always afraid it's gonna get really bad and kill me. I'm so scared of it."

Paul suddenly and forcefully clapped his hands together: "Scared to DEATH, baby! Whoop! Whoop!"

"*Fuck*, you're a dick!" Jim snapped.

"Little little boopie," Paul rejoined as he moved in to cuddle Jim's face. "*Little* little boo-pee-pie. Cutie boopboop."

Jim guffawed, fending off Paul with a reluctant smile. "Stop.

Get off me."

Paul kissed Jim on the forehead. "Let's go get this boopster married."

It Turned Out that Reality Was Overrated

There's nothing romantic about Sartre. You read Sartre and you're on your own, no two ways about it. The world is at a distance, separate, outside. Ah, but I remember the time of García Márquez, undergraduate nights when a bunch of us would sit around drunk and talk about passion and empathy, that real empathy by which you vibrate correspondingly with another, even if only fleetingly. I remember Hemingway and Kerouac, I remember suffering for art and the ideal. It wasn't always a happy life, but it was full of feeling, meaning. It was not that sterile, living, doctoral death of Camus and Beckett, absurd and cold and why bother at all, really? There is something to be said for romance, for wallowing in pain and misery, for knowing you're alive, whatever it means, no matter how illusory. *Being and Nothingness.* Christ. What a world.

Can't Help But See

I see why she wants to draw them. The clouds are a tableau of swirl and roll that's catching an impossible luminous pink.

They're turning smoke gray from east to west, it's just the edges now but you know it's coming, you can see it happening if you watch carefully enough. She's sketching madly, outline, shading, colored pencils pressed into service then dropped on one another with a gentle tinkling. She has these eyes like you've never seen, they're bigger than her head, they pivot with a flow and force that you can almost hear, those synched-up chasms that would express emotion even where there is none (while she brushes her teeth, when she's dead in the morgue). They seem to take in more photons than yours or mine or anybody's, trying to trap more than their fair share of the light that flashes by, so much so that you'd swear you see them glowing, nothing figurative about it. She looks from sky to sketch pad to sky again, trying so hard to create something fully true to what she sees out there and what she is in there before it's gone. It's desperate, impossible but she tries so hard, the clouds now half dark and half more impossible pink than ever and so deep that you want them to explode or melt and hope that's what the end will look like. I see why she wants to draw them, but if you just saw those eyes you might forget for a second that there's color or clouds or a sky there at all for all that trying, trying, trying, you might forget that there's nothing you can do but look.

[Wait and see.]

Teeth and Other Things

"I'd love some."

Every time the waitress smiled at him, he could not help noticing that her right-front incisor was crooked, angling towards its twin so severely it appeared to be artificial, as if it were on the mouth of a grotesque Halloween mask. He fixed his eyes on hers, forcing himself to smile. *Does she think I'm staring?* She turned to cut the piece of lemon meringue pie he had ordered. *Jesus, I am staring. But fuck, can you blame me?*

A comely blonde woman at the end of the counter had been watching him since he had arrived, and she suppressed a laugh at his grimace. She took a final sip of her coffee, then scribbled a note on a napkin: *Can you believe that tooth?!*

"Cindy, could you come in here a minute?"

She rolled her chair from the reception desk and, after a sigh, stood and walked into his office, closing the door behind her. *Why does he have to be with that black girl?* she thought. *God damn it.*

He sat down behind his desk, perusing a chart fastened to the inside of a manila folder. "It looks like we better go ahead and take 12 out now. And 14 is going to need a filling." But Cindy's attention was on the photograph (to the right of his nameplate: DR. DAVID SANTIAGO, D.D.S.), on that black girl, Diamond.

"Listen, Phil, this is a goddamn serious proposal."

Philip Norville was running out of patience. He was sweating through his dress shirt and angry at himself for letting his longtime friend drag him out to a desolate patch of flatland in the middle of the afternoon. "Jesus, Rob, just think about it for a second." He clicked his teeth together and felt a sharp pain on the right side of his mouth. *Oh, shit, not that filling again.*

Robert Stanley Singer III could stand nothing less than having his comprehension questioned, an overcompensation for his belief (correct, as it turned out) that much of what happened in the world, and even in his own life, was beyond his ken. "Listen, goddamn it: the start-up wouldn't be more than $20 million. We put together the consortium, we bid on the land . . . I mean, it's good for everyone, right? Now, look at these numbers." Singer bent down and opened his briefcase, retrieving a yellow legal pad. Norville read the words that had been scribbled almost illegibly at the top: *Fiscal breakdown of Arena Plan.*

"Nah, nothing so far today."

The man listened to the response that came through the receiver, a smile spreading across his face until he laughed out loud, his steel-rimmed sunglasses reflecting a wavering beam of sunlight across the room as he slowly nodded his head. *I'd like to get in between your thighs*, he thought.

He rubbed his forehead with the back of his free hand as he heard the words coming across a telephone line suspended high above the dirt and desiccated brush that constituted the area's landscape. He looked at a poster pinned against a wood-paneled wall: a caricature of a squat, smiling Mexican, including huge sombrero and mouthful of rotting teeth, lined up in crosshairs. There was a caption at the bottom: *Spic Insight*.

"Flight 619—Dallas/Fort Worth nonstop to Los Angeles—now boarding at Gate C14."

The little girl clung more tightly to her mother's hand. *What's Los Angeles?* she thought.

"Mommy, what's Los Angeles?" But her mother, Carol, was engulfed in a heated conversation with her boyfriend. The little girl waited for a reply, and when it did not come, her gaze wandered the terminal along which she was being pulled. She read the sign above the area toward which the three were heading: *Gate C14*. She moved her tongue against her only remaining top incisor, rocking it slowly from front to back and back to front.

"Come on. Is this for real?"

He scanned the parking lot, searching for the blonde, but she was nowhere to be seen. *Why the fuck did she give me this stupid note?* A gust of wind blew a tumbleweed across the dusty asphalt. *Fucking Abilene. Stupid country hicks. Figures.*

"Cindy, are you all right?"

She opened her eyes, saw the ceiling. Her right hand pressed the floor. *Oh my God, I'm so embarrassed. Of all the places to faint in Tyler.* She looked into David's eyes and could see that his concern was genuine but clinical, professional, no ring of love, not even the worry of one friend for another. Evoked by a gentle gale, the architecture of Dr. Santiago's Dental Office gave a plaintive howl that Cindy alone took in. *What's wrong with me?*

"Phil, are you paying attention?"

Norville reached into his mouth with right thumb and forefinger, retrieved the loosened gold, tarnished metal, worthless hunk of earth. He tossed it down; a short breeze covered it. *What an asshole*, he thought, gazing at his partner. "Rob, sure, Dallas and Houston are thriving, but that doesn't mean the league is going to just hand Austin a fucking franchise. And you wanna invest with strangers?" He turned his head and spat, half-expecting to see blood. "You know, you really are an A-hole sometimes."

"See ya later, doll."

The border guard set the receiver down in its cradle and stood up. He picked up the rifle that was leaning against the desk and stepped towards the door. He felt a warm breeze blow across his leathery face as he emerged from the small shack of an office.

Come on, you fucking wetbacks. Just you try me today.

"Mommy, my tooth came out! Mommy!"

Carol broke off in mid-sentence and stooped. "Oh wow, baby!" She looked down, right, snatched the tiny enamel chip from the terminal's flat carpeting. "Here," she said, pressing it on tiny palm. "Los Angeles is the place where we're going so you can visit your daddy. We're going to go through that door and get on that airplane outside there, and then we'll FLY fly fly through the air to Los Angeles to see your daddy." She kissed her daughter on the cheek, stood, resumed the argument while they took their places in the boarding line. The little girl looked at the airliner through the glass wall to the left side of the gate, then at a Styrofoam cup blown over the nose of the plane by a circular current of air. *I hope the tooth fairy will be able to find me at my daddy's at Los Angeles*, her internal voice chimed. She looked at her mother's boyfriend. *I can't wait to see my daddy.* She looked back out at the airliner. The Styrofoam cup was gone.

Comeback

Not as a fish, I said, or I don't know, maybe it would depend on the fish, I don't know, probably not. It would be whatever's conscious, whatever has subjective experience, feels—there's no *sum* without *cogito*. Yes, as a dolphin, I said, a whale, a chimpanzee, not a bug I'm sure, but a cat, a dog. You come back not as O Heavenly Dog or something but Benji as Benji. You accumulate that, your soul ages, acquires. I don't know how what you come back as is determined, maybe it's random, probably not but otherwise it could get a little moralistic for this ontology. But your soul (whatever it is) soaks up the experience, each experience, and you keep coming back until you've taken in enough, until boredom or disgust or satiety tells you it's all the same or that it doesn't matter or there's been too much repetition, that you're tired of being so locked away from everything all the time, I don't know. You wouldn't have access to your previous lives except in the void, where you choose to leave or finally stay.

Jesus, you said, fuck that! What good does it do me to come back as not-me me? Acquisition of experience? Okay, so there's all kind of variation out there, everything is unique and confined to its own sum, whatever the fuck, okay. Let me just be me and extrapolate from there, let me just be me and presume the otherness and generate compassion from my presumption. When I come back—and I will, you do again and again—I'll be me, my experience, my life as me, Chevy Chase in the dog's body or whatever you said each time around, living it again and again, woof, I'm that Heavenly Dog here for another chance to improve on my life. Or I'm the exact same Heavenly Dog having the exact same wacky earthly adventure—the same predicaments and danger, the same tugging at your heartstrings, the exact same climax and happy ending. I'll accumulate it, like you say, I'm accumulating it right now, each time something different, my soul picking up a little more of the experience, each time a little more, a little better grasp of what's happening here, and I'll never be finished, like a permanent museum exhibit I keep revisiting to better understand it or see it anew. Because it's not like *Groundhog Day* for a life you don't remember living. I want to know what I did here, I want to hold on to everything. That's why I love you, you said kissing me once, twice: everything you do I take in and remember, every moment with you makes a permanent impression, I feel it now and it's with me always.

Selected Philosophical Terms

A, B, C, etc.
> the attempt to label, to differentiate, to explain, to impart (an attempt that often fails spectacularly)

being
> "[...] There is nothing in heaven or on earth which does not contain in itself being and nothingness."
> —GEORG WILHELM FRIEDRICH HEGEL

cogito ergo sum
> all that one can truly know

Darstellung
> representation

Ding an sich
  a thing in itself (as if this were possible)

Erlebnis
  experience, experiencing (n.)

Erlebnisse
  experiences

Esperanto
  a hopeful but ultimately futile attempt at a universal language (cp. ESPERANZADO)

exist
  to be in this (or any) world

experience
  "Experience, already reduced to a swarm of impressions, is ringed round for each one of us by that thick wall of personality through which no real voice has ever pierced on its way to us, or from us to that which we can only conjecture to be without."   —WALTER PATER

far
  a measure of distance and of extension

Jungian archetypes
  proof of interconnectedness (a hopeful definition)

mauvaise foi
  "bad faith"; self-deception; the most insidious of traps

neurons
  nerve cells found not just in the brain, but also the heart; not much good on their own, but when they network, wow!

nothingness
  "[...] In order for a _self_ to exist, it is necessary that the unity of this being include its own nothingness as a nihilation of identity."   —JEAN-PAUL SARTRE

pain

"Some intense stimuli trigger reflex withdrawal, auto-
nomic responses and pain."

> —WIKIPEDIA (from NOCICEPTOR), an artifact
> of the early 21st century, "a free encyclo-
> pedia, written synergistically by the people
> who use it"

philosophical terms

words used in the attempt to express something, nothing
more

remember

"Remembering is not the re-excitation of innumerable
fixed, lifeless and fragmentary traces. It is an imaginative
reconstruction, or construction, built out of the relation of
our attitude towards a whole active mass of organized past
reactions or experience and to a little outstanding detail
which commonly appears in image or language form. It is
thus hardly ever really exact, even in the most rudi-
mentary cases of rote recapitulation, and it is not at all
important that it should be so."

> —SIR FREDERIC BARTLETT

selected

the choices we have made

signifier

that which represents

Verständigung

process of communication (a, the)

Vorstellungen

representations

"wait and see"

an idiom (short for *Wait and you will see*) usually
employed to mean *You may doubt, but your doubt will be*

answered, etc. Interestingly, *wait and see* as autotelium (i.e., not short for anything) posits a novel (and perhaps unattainable) temporal status, namely, the suspended hopeful present (cp. ESPERAR) married to the realized (because promised) future (cp. ECCO, EUREKA). What happens to the past in such a state is a secondarily interesting question.

wall

    a painfully obvious symbol (apropos as it may be)

woof/weft

1. threads interwoven with one another to make a single fabric (e.g., cashmere)
2. words lovers say to one another when the world is as close to perfect as it could ever get

What the Might-Have-Been Meesus Said about Self-Representation

    She liked to tell the story of telling her a priori grief counselor (helping her mourn her coming loss) a story about a visit to the dentist, about a moment she felt a slight twinge of pain, light, an instant, a trepidation, ah, a mental flinch, Is the anesthetic wearing off. "Did you notice that the pain was in a straight line?" he asked her, gesturing towards his jaw, middle finger wagging to describe a line of longitude. Yes, she said with the wonder of recognition, that's right. "It represents as . . . even though the nerves aren't . . . because really there's, you know, a tangle." That was a piece of a puzzle, she said. It had always concerned her, and here it was. Her counselor looked pleased. Mouse was sure she must have, too.

Husband, Father Killed by Drunk Driver

The garage door's hinges were quiet, smooth. It floated upwards, gliding, feather-light. Lee's left hand lingered as he took in the sight of his EID-650, new, the odometer not yet showing triple-digits, the white plastic, the racing stripes forest green and black and forest green, the gas tank's silver cap, the black and metal underpinnings, the stubby Plexiglas windscreen, the fresh rubber of the tires. He felt vibrant, comfortably corporeal, fit and master of a new machine. He was particularly gauged into his physical existence because of his throat—not sore or raw but a bit off, noticeable. He was ever so slightly fatigued, which could be nothing or perhaps the onset of a cold. He stepped around the front of the house the way he had come and entered. His wife looked up from the kitchen table (his daughter remaining focused on her dessert).

"Forget something, hun?"

"Yeah."

He strode down the hallway and into the master bedroom. He went directly to his dresser and opened the top drawer, felt around briefly, located the open roll of lozenges. He thumbed one into a hand and popped it into his mouth. He did not suck hard candy for pleasure (he had lost his childhood taste for gumballs and Certs), but the chemical cherry flavor was always enjoyable at first. He slid the drawer shut and reversed his course, again passing the breakfast nook.

"Bye."

"Have a good time," his wife drawled for the second time in the last five minutes. Their daughter was feeding herself another spoonful of melting Neapolitan ice cream (which all three called "the pink-brown-white").

The taste was cloying. He resisted the temptation to bite down and be done with it because the zinc really did seem to work, he had no idea why. I've never sucked a lozenge while wearing a helmet, he thought, I've never experienced this before. He swung his right leg over the bike and moved the weight off the kickstand, mounting his possession. He kick-started the engine; it rolled into a gentle staccato chug. He raised the sonic tone with an almost imperceptible dropping of his right wrist; the engine hummed into his body. The cherry flavor was upon him.

Man and machine glided down his street, down another, wound through his neighborhood and out into more commercial zones, in perfect synchrony, machine and man. The lozenge was tiresome, still nearly its original size. He felt the urge to spit it out. The yellow minivan swerved violently, into him, he toppled, tumbled.

The horror was immediate and overwhelming. For a stretch of time horror and suffering were all. Then a process—simple, almost mechanical, quiet, not consciously him—pieced together a sense of his reality: his throat, the agony and fear, choking, you cannot swallow, you cannot inhale. The flavor was pain now, the awareness, the chemical cherry, his desperate tongue stained with taste. He could not consider any further, could not register that his body was only bruised and scraped, could not organize himself well enough to stand. He flailed his arms and legs, a bulky insect flipped onto its shell, reduced, primal defeat. His visual system filtered down to a still-human patch of consciousness that he was being attended to, but he was beyond their reach now, beyond hearing Are you okay, Don't move him, Somebody call 9-1-1.

The Sick and the Dying

I have the flu. I hate it when I'm sick. It seems so pointless, it's a waste. I just sit here and do nothing. I'm waiting, I guess, waiting for it to pass. It doesn't matter that I won't have much more to do when I'm well—it's just stupid to be sick. I always feel sorry for myself. It's not so much for the sickness, because it's the flu, I'm not suffering terribly. I think it's just that I can't do anything, that I just sit here, stewing in a general unpleasantness, waiting. I'm sick, I think, I don't feel good, feel well. I lie down, not even hoping to sleep, just lying there, I'm sick, I don't feel well. When I'm sick it feels so stupid, like I ought to either be well or die. Something so in between doesn't serve any purpose. You should be well, and then when you start to feel otherwise it should be the end, that's it, I'm dying, it's over, I felt okay but now it's over. I wouldn't mind that so much, the process, it would be new, what they call novel, a one-time-only thing. Of course I wouldn't like it, of course I'd be scared, but I'd know it was the end, that it was all coming to an end, that I was heading for something, nearing it, even if it was just nothing, the end. This stupid flu, sitting here, I'm sick, that's all, it's dumb.

I wish I hadn't killed those women. It's not that I feel guilty so much, but I didn't have to do it. I remember how it all built up, I remember the first time I hit one. She looked so good, that whore, and I was talking to her and she was so full of herself, and I just wanted to hit her, and I hit her, and it felt so good, and I hit her again, hard, I saw the blood coming out of her nose, and I couldn't believe I'd done it, and I felt like I was overflowing, and I ran. That overflowing felt so good and I wanted more, I wanted to go with it, I wanted to overflow, to keep going, but I ran, I didn't know what to do and I ran, I ran and screamed and laughed. I'd felt it welled up inside me before, but to be able to do it, to do it, to hit one, to just hit her in the face, to realize it, to let it come, it felt so good. I was running down the street and just laughing every now and then, like a sob I couldn't stop but it was a laugh. *I did it*, I thought, *I hit her, I hit her right in the face*, and I laughed. I was running so hard and I could barely breathe, but the sob-laugh kept coming, *I can't believe I did it, I hurt her, I saw the blood*, it felt so good. I remember being at home, sitting on my bed and thinking about it, it felt so good, I wanted more, I knew I could do it again, I knew I could go farther, *I could do anything*, like I could go all the way.

I don't think I could ever make anyone understand. They'd think it was all about hating them and wanting them to suffer, but that had nothing to do with it, or not too much. I just hit her and it felt so good. I'd always had the urge, but when I did it it was like nothing I could have imagined, the rush, the power. It wasn't a physical power or dominance, because I knew I wasn't strong, but it was the power to do something, to change something, to extend myself out there. I hit her, and I just wanted to keep hitting her. It's amazing I hit her only twice, I don't know how I stopped, how I pulled myself away. I saw the blood, I'd hit her nose and the sound, knowing that suddenly there was pain and shock. But that she felt pain, that it hurt her, that she was scared, that she didn't know what was happening or what was coming, that she couldn't think, couldn't even react, I almost regretted that. I wanted to do it again, do it more, but I wished I could feel the way I did when I hit her without her feeling like that, like if I could just hit her and she would change, would plunge toward death somehow, would be changed and I'd be hitting her and breaking her and feeling like I did and that she'd feel it but was okay with it, was going somewhere and just accepting it, even if it were unpleasant. It's like with my flu now: if it were the ending it'd be okay, even though I feel bad. If it could be like that for her and I could let it come, let myself be carried away, that would be heaven. I knew it could never quite be like that, but I couldn't control that. I wanted to feel it again, to feel it more, to feel it all the way, and that was all. I could only worry about me.

I must have sweat more in the time leading up to the first one than I'd sweat in all of the rest of my life till then. It was like I had a fever on the outside. I wanted it so bad I ached. I knew it was going to happen, but I had to make it happen. It was there, and I just had to push it over the edge. Every time I'd see a woman in the right place I'd want to do it, but it was like I wasn't ready, like I knew I didn't have my plans in order, even though I didn't really need any plans. I don't know what I was waiting for,

I wasn't waiting for anything really, except maybe when it started to come, like floating down a river, floating for awhile, then speeding up, then hearing a different sound and knowing a waterfall was a coming. When I was there, I would just let it carry me over, let it flow and fall and overcome everything.

I was with one in the alley, and it was quiet. The walls looked black in places because there wasn't much light, but I could see their roughness, the unevenness of the surface of that type of brick, the thin trail of still water in the gutter in the middle of the alleyway. I could hear water drip in various places, I heard a car drive past the end of the alley, I felt it coming, I felt like the car was bearing down on me but it had gone, there was no car but just a feeling like that. I looked at her, the extra makeup, the frizzed-out hair, the rough walls, and there was an alkaline taste in my mouth, and I punched her so hard, I punched her again, in the stomach this time, she grunted, one arm went across her stomach and the other tried to fight me off, her ass bumped the wall, it must have felt rough against her tight cotton skirt. I hit her again, on the back of the neck, it was a bad place to hit someone but I didn't know what to do, I felt joy, I was overcome with it, I hit her and hit her, I barely knew what I was doing, I kneed her face, then grabbed her head and shoved it against the wall. I kissed her hard, I don't know why, just right quick, ramming my head into her forehead, it hurt but I didn't care, she couldn't breathe or talk but she was crying a little, it was happening fast, I punched her in the chest, I hit her tits, I aimed a punch at one, hitting it so hard, I punched her in the throat, she made a croak, I kneed her cunt, I hit her three or four times in the same place, quick, her stomach or lower, her womb, I threw her on the ground and fell on her, ramming my elbows on her, my forearm on her throat, I don't know what else, it must have hurt so much, but then she was dead, I don't know when but it was obvious at some point. It was like the ride was over but the thrill was staying with me, like feeling like I was still on the roller-coaster while walking to another ride. I had never felt so good in my life. I felt like the rest of my life would be different, like I was empowered, like I was unassailable, like I was immortal, like I was in heaven and would be there for eternity, like I had just found out I was an angel and I'd be here forever, I'm in heaven, life is over and I'm in heaven, here I am, in heaven, everything is fine, everything was glowing as I went on walking down the street, everything was reaching out to me, embracing me. I loved everything, and everything loved me. We were in harmony. It felt like that was forever.

When I woke up the next morning I still felt good, but not good like I did the night before. I loved that I'd done it. I couldn't believe it. I felt waves of pride, but I knew it wasn't like what I'd felt last night. The rest of the day was okay, but I couldn't make myself believe that I felt as good as I had the night before. When I went to bed that night I didn't feel well, I knew it was slipping away, I was afraid to sleep, and the next morning it was nearly gone, almost to like I hadn't done it. I couldn't stand it, and I knew it was going to get worse, that everything was going to go back to like it was, and it was obvious that I had to do it again. For some reason I didn't want to, but I knew I had to. I felt like I was a vampire that has a soul and a conscience but he has to feed, and he has to feed in his way. I didn't like what she must have felt, how it must have hurt. I thought about getting hit like that, and I knew it would be terrible. I waited for awhile, and I was sweating again, but it wasn't the same, it wasn't anxiousness or anticipation now but pain, like withdrawal maybe a little bit, and it got worse as time went on. I was so relieved when the other one was coming back to my apartment, she wanted to have sex with me, and I looked at her in the passenger seat and she looked at me and smiled, and I thought, *You're going to die, you're going to die*, and I smiled, and it hurt and felt good, and I had to feed. We got inside and I was sweating so much again, and I asked her if she wanted something to drink, and I brought her something, I don't even know what, and she drank it, and I watched her, and she put it down and looked at me. We were sitting on the couch and she was ready to kiss, and I looked at her and I hit her across the face, she flailed weakly a couple of times, and I clawed at her throat and started punching her tits, so hard, and she sounded like an animal but it was too late to fight, and I was being swept away, falling over the waterfall with the water hugging me and welcoming me, bearing me into heaven, I ripped at her face, her jaw must've come out of socket or something, she bleated like a goat as I dug at her eyes, and she was blind and bleeding and dying and suffering and scared, and I wonder if she thought about her parents, thought about not being able to say goodbye, and I smashed her into the coffee table and it broke, and I stomped on her head, and she went all limp but was still alive, I could tell, and I kicked at her spine, kicked it and kicked it, and I loved everything, the world was singing to me. I felt the glow of everything, I looked around and I knew how loud everything had been but I didn't care, I sat on the couch and just felt, and everything was perfect. It was over, and I was in heaven, I was an angel, everything loved me and I was a part of it all and so far away from anything here.

I wish I hadn't killed those women. I even wish I hadn't hit the other one. I don't feel bad about it, and it's not prison or anything. It's just that it's so pointless, like the flu. I felt good then, I did it, but so what? They died and they're gone, and I'm here, and their families and friends are here, I saw them in court. I didn't care about what they said, but they're here, in this world with me, and that lasts, it lasts like how I felt when I did it didn't last, so what was the point? I remember what I did, but I don't get to feel it, I just remember feeling it, so what lasts is not something I know how to use, and it's bad for them, these people I don't know and don't care about but don't hate and it doesn't help me if they feel bad. I know what it's like to feel bad, not like those women did but they're gone, they were going somewhere, going to the end, and so if they'd just known that like I'd know if this flu were a one-time-only deal and then you die, that would have been okay, but I couldn't make them know that, which is too bad, and now their families and friends are here and feel bad, which is so pointless, like a flu that never goes away, it's so pointless and I'm sorry to be a part of that. And so if I just hadn't killed them it wouldn't matter to me now, I wouldn't be any worse off, I didn't get anything I know how to use now, so it just would have been better not to ever have done it. But I did, and I have the flu, and I won't die after it but I'll get better, and then I'll sit here and watch TV and look at magazines and wait. If someone would just come in here and kill me now, just fucking walk in and shoot me in the head, it would be better, it would be less pointless than waiting, letting me get better and waiting for my execution. But there's nothing I can do about it. The flu is a stupid thing, and living is a waste, and that's all.

Call Him Jim

I knew this guy, I forget his name, it doesn't matter what I call him, he is what he is, which has nothing to do with his name/label/what have you. Maybe I call him Jim, "Jim" can stand for him or somebody else, two differences called the same, made the same, a hundred, a million, more. Jim could be a brother or a boopie, a boopie more or less. He was Jim, he wasn't Jim, Jim wasn't Jim, this Jim, that Jim, this love for another whom you can never know, that what in your chest you're afraid will close in, neither love nor pain, awake and asleep, pixie mouse baby, just this or that, a flickering something that labels never touch. Hi, Jim. Bye, Jim.

Rain

As he awoke he heard inhumanly rapid tapping all around, the waves of increase and decrease along the roof shingles, the steady pinging of individual drops finding their ways onto something inside the walls, metal presumably.

"Crap," he said.

[Wait and see.]

The No

"Mouse, wake up. It's time to get up."

"I'm not going."

"What do you mean, Mouse?"

"I'm not doing it anymore. It's pointless."

"Come on, Mouse. Let's get out of bed."

"No. No more."

"Terry, you can't give up now. I know—"

"Fuck, Dad, it's pointless! God damn it! I'm fucking dying, okay? Fucking deal with it. Jesus."

"— . . ."

"Dad, Daddy, stop. Don't cry. I'm sorry. I didn't mean to yell. And I'm sorry, but it's true. You know it. I just . . . I don't want to go through it anymore. Look at me, my hair . . . *Look at this!* And inside, I feel like I'm being poisoned, Daddy, and that's what it is. This isn't me. This isn't *life*. It is what it is, Dad. We're just pretending, we're just playing at something. I . . . I can't. I won't. It's okay. Shhh, Daddy. C'mere. Shhhh, shhhh."

Embellishment (a poem reconsidered)

Had we actually been out in the rain
it might have gone differently.
But we were on the sidewalk,
under an awning.

[Keep looking.]

"I don't want it to end this way," she said.
She looked at me, her eyes like a second voice
saying, "I don't want it to end this way."
I was looking out at the street where

the rain fell, anticipating how powerful
it would feel to deny her. "Nevertheless,"
I said, "this is the way it ends."
I even touched her cheek.

Walking home I remembered a blue glass.
It was a favorite of hers, a gift
from her sister, and I remembered how
after dropping it I itched with distress,

those blue fragments looking up
from the white kitchen tile, and she
laughing, saying not to worry,
not to worry.

Life That Never Is

To be in the midst of life, this life, this strange fucking life
that never is but becomes and has become, to be in it, for it to
happen around me, flowing, and my being a part, at least of that
flow. I know it's all connected, or so I presume, a nice thought,
whatever the case. It's so strange, strange that people don't seem
to question it, not many, in the least, at least to say this thing, this
entire thing, this whole fragmented thing that I call life, it's here,
still and lumbering like a dumb beast, insensible animal, a
leviathan, beast that blots out everything, beast in the middle of
nothingness, dropped on top, inserted, fucked, rutting like a beast,

stagnant, gigantic, consuming. I look at it there, out there, knowing that I'm a part, an organ, less important, a lesser component, a cell, I'm a cell. We, an assembly of cells that sings of itself, we vary, we live and die, we are the body but the body remains unchanged relative to us, too macro- to our microcosm, it's just here, insensate, a thing, an unconscious totality. It's what doesn't matter because it doesn't care, it's lower than an animal, baser than a beast, and we ourselves, the only thing we know, the entirety of our direct experience, we sacrifice ourselves, we offer ourselves up on the altar of this nothing, illusion, we lie down for the slaughter and our blood just runs, it doesn't write a message, it doesn't have meaning, it just drips and flows.

Place Names and Places B

AMSTERDAM, capital and most populous city of the Netherlands. Built on polders, then brutally occupied by Nazi Germany 1940–1945, Amsterdam is now one of the most affluent cities in all of Europe and a major tourist destination. Canals, cannabis, and so much more!

BALAZIC (from *Bella Zig*, "Land of Beautiful Lines"), an isolated island whose only export is poetry.

CASABLANCA, symbol of modern Morocco and its main metropolis and seaport. Beginning in the early 20th century,

Casablanca was built up by the occupying French around the old Moorish city. Site of the Casablanca Conference of January 1943, at which U.S. President Franklin D. Roosevelt and British Prime Minister Winston Churchill pledged that their two nations would fight the good fight until German Reich Chancellor Adolf Hitler (author of MEIN KAMPF) and the Axis powers surrendered unconditionally. Come visit the tourist hotspot of Northern Africa!

KASHMIR, a disputed mountain region in a faraway land.

A Few Remains

When we re-met, she sitting on a bench near faculty parking, holding her finger with a napkin, a decent amount of blood, she'd scratched herself but it was nothing, she was fine, how was I doing today, oh my God, *Perry?* That she missed her parents, she wasn't sure whether she really loved them but she missed them. That she had inherited from her mother the love of leaving notes for strangers. That time she laughed just when I was about to cry, "Life is so absurd" she said, "so fucking stupid." She was laughing, "It's ridiculous," and I felt interrupted, embarrassed, but I cried, laughing while I cried, and how it felt good to be in that place with her. And the way she looked at me then, not sure it was okay, still laughing, "Fucking life, piece of shit," laughing, I cried and laughed.

That all the Cure songs she could name had three-word titles: *Close to Me, Just Like Heaven, Pictures of You, Boys Don't Cry.* That she loved the idea of dancing but was too self-conscious ever to do it, even when she was alone, she knew it was stupid, she hated it but she couldn't let go like that, she didn't know why, didn't know how to figure it out. That she preferred pot to booze but hated tea, how that was surely common enough but to me seemed so uniquely her. Where on her ribs she loved to be touched just before she came, how I loved to do it, the sound she'd make and how it felt to feel her make it, to know that I had made her make it, made her feel like that, her, like that. That she never remembered what she had given me as Christmas or birthday gifts, "When did you get this" she would ask holding up a favorite book of hers (and subsequently mine). The last time I saw her, what she said and the way she looked, with the sun behind her, my leaving so she could not leave me, the feel of the air and the taste of my own mouth.

These, a few others, not much else.

Art Appreciation 101 (Early 21st Century)

PIXIES, (The), American musical group. Charles Michael Kittridge Thompson IV, Kim Deal, David Lovering, Joey

Santiago. (Individually they have also been/been called/ called themselves: Black Francis/Frank Black, Mrs. John Murphy, Dave, Joe, &c.) Guitars (electric, acoustic, bass), drums, occasionally other instruments, and voices (primarily in English, sometimes in Spanish, occasionally in no language at all) intertwined in various ways to create musical compositions (songs) and collections of songs (albums). Aided by producers (e.g., GIL NORTON), engineers, etc. Heard and seen in various media: compact disc (CD), digital video disc (DVD), magnetic tape, vinyl, radio, television, Internet, in person, others. Begun in BOSTON, MA, in 1986. Officially disbanded 1993. Reunited 2004. Musical influences: DAVID BOWIE (British musical artist; "Ashes to ashes, funk to funky / We know Major Tom's a junkie [...] Hitting an all-time low"), LOU REED (American musical artist; "And something flickered for a minute / And then it vanished and was gone"), THE CURE (British musical group; "No one ever knows or loves another"), et al. (Bands influenced by include MODEST MOUSE, b. 1993. Sample lyric: "We have one chance, one chance to get everything right / In heaven, everything is fine.") Other influences: film (e.g., *Un chien andalou*, *Eraserhead*), art in general, THE UNITED STATES, THE WORLD, life, and so forth. Sample lyric: "Bam thwok, (oh) love, bang, crash, wokka wokka / In heaven, everything is fine."

Once During Lovemaking (Another Time, Another Place)

Uh, said the man to the lady.

This is right now. This is right now.

I love you, he said.

Right now this is right now

I love you, he said.

whatever is to come, this is right now, right now, right now

Nature vs. Nurture

"Let's cut through the golf course," Mitch said. "I don't wanna go all the way around."

"We'll get hassled," Abe said. "Man, those fucking tight-asses. I don't wanna deal with it."

"Come on," Debra chirped, bopping between them from behind.

"But I don't wanna get hit by a golf ball. We almost got beaned the last time."

Mitch gestured at the dark gray sky. "No one's golfing right now. It's gonna start pouring. It's drizzling already. No one's playing golf today. No problemo." He peeled back the thick sheet of ivy, revealing their hole in the chain-link fencing, and Debra slipped through. Mitch waited on Abe like a faithful doorman. "Coming?"

"Fuck," Abe muttered as he ducked through. Mitch curled behind him, the ivy falling back into place with a few small bounces that Mitch heard but did not notice.

The three teens were clad in matching black trench coats, and they could hardly have been more conspicuous jogging across fairways and greens. They crested gentle hills and frolicked down into miniature valleys, jockeying each other and laughing, not a golfer to be seen.

At a long incline they slowed to a walk. As they reached the plateau Mitch rolled onto the uniformly stubby grass. "Woooo! I'm a rock-and-roller! Woooo!"

"What are you doing," Abe asked dubiously.

"I'm rocking and rolling! Woooo! Hey," Mitch said, eyeing a range ball about 30 feet away. He jogged over and dove on it, then rose to one knee. "Go out for a pass," he motioned, cocking his right arm and beckoning Abe away with his left. "Go long." Finally Abe obliged, and Mitch gently lobbed the ball in front of him. "Dive!" he yelled.

Abe was no Jerry Rice, no Steve Largent, and the dimpled globe bounced off his right forearm as he flopped to the turf, then rolled demonstratively onto his back.

Debra could not catch her breath, enjoying herself so profoundly that for a moment she forgot her sadness over how boys this beautiful could never love her.

A deafening crack sharply echoed from everywhere. For a moment impossible to quantify, Abe and Mitch could see absolutely nothing but white. Finally they came to themselves, regaining an equilibrium.

"What the fuck," Mitch yelled over his tinnitus, stiff with tension and adrenaline, not quite registering the rumbling of the sky. "Holy shit!"

"Holy fuck," Abe called. "Holy goddamn fuck!"

"What happened," Mitch yelled.

Abe and Mitch looked at each other, then at Debra.

She remained, unmoving, dazed. Her pink hoop earrings were nowhere in sight; a wisp of smoke sedately rose from her scalp. Her companions ran to her, calling her name, but each stopped short and looked her up and down, both inclined to touch her, both balking.

"Debra," Mitch said, "Debra! Debra! Are you okay?"

"Debra, are you okay? Can you hear me?"

Mitch jabbed at her arm. "Debra!"

She looked at him absently.

Abe gently touched her elbow. "Debra, hey, are you okay?"

Slowly she turned to him.

"Debra. Debra. Say something."

"Whoaaaaaa," she said.

"Debra, are you okay?"

"Fuuuuuuuuuck," she replied, smiling in amazement. "Oh my God, dude. Fuck."

"Are you okay," Abe asked. Mitch began to laugh. "What are you laughing at, you idiot?"

"Fuuuuck," Debra said with a nervous titter. Mitch was laughing in fits now. "Dude, I got hit by lightning."

"*Woooo*," Mitch screamed, "*woo-hoooooo!*" He took Debra by the hand, and they bounded towards the clubhouse. Abe watched for a moment, then followed their lead. The rain began to come down hard, and they screamed and ran and laughed.

Greetings from Amsterdam

Hi Mom, Dad, and Christopher!

You were right—Amsterdam is incredible! I haven't been here for two hours and I'm already in love! The streets, the canals—and I haven't even GONE anywhere yet! I'm down in a coffeeshop (no, not a coffeeshop) not too far from our hotel.

Our hotel! We've got this room at the Museum Hotel. It's right on the corner of the third floor. Out one window we look across to the Rijksmuseum, out the other we look down on a canal.

It's hard, though. We had just checked in, and the three of us were raving about the room, and then Gina just started to cry. As you can imagine, that was enough to get Opal and I going, and we all just lost it. I can't believe this is really happening. I don't know if we're going to be able to hold it together the whole time. I'm glad we got here a day before the others (except for Perry). Hopefully this will give us a chance to get used to it. We want to be strong for Terry. Knowing her, though, she'll be the one being strong for the rest of us. I'm going to focus on the positive, though, and stay in the now, and make it good. I'm happy to be here . . . even if I'm sad inside.

Love,

E.

My Struggle, It's Nothing

I'm tormented by the idea that it's all nothing. I accept that things exist—coffee, Casablanca, you, your favorite songs—and I allow for their valuations, subjective as they may be, that things matter or they don't, are wholly good or wholly bad or fall somewhere in between. But what is a single death or the Holocaust to water or Saturn's rings, to the expanse of time and space, within which we may as well never have existed? What is tomorrow's ecstasy or horror to yesterday? Moments come and go, things happen and stop happening, that's all. I spend half my time trying to turn this nothing into something, to capture and preserve it, to bring life to lifeless dust. This is nothing, I keep saying, but here it is. Look, it's nothing, look.

Jack Valenti Is Near Death (One of Our Jokes) ®

G—GENERAL AUDIENCES. All Ages Admitted. ®

PG—PARENTAL GUIDANCE SUGGESTED. SOME MATERIAL MAY NOT BE SUITABLE FOR CHILDREN. ®

PG-13—PARENTS STRONGLY CAUTIONED. Some Material May Be Inappropriate for Children Under 13. ®

Remission

The rain I drift my house is under a waterfall. The water breaks hard the roof shingles turgid and leaking overcrowded sponges She darts upright There's someone there You are my friend the voice subhumanly low quietslams my ears She is asleep The rain falls hard a shufflingshe is upright in rigid shaking shock head turning circles her neck will not allow her hair fans the wind wings of a trapped bird There's someone out there I saw a face in the I look nothing but her asleep next to I turn my back close my eyes the room tips up on one corner sitting up shescreams a piercing whistle through the flat room I cannot breathe the agony her fleering jawbone swaying side to side her chin touching her ears a fleer beneath her glowing bleeding eyes and tongue snakeflicking smile the scream never tapering she lunges a bite out of my chest my throat windpipe my lungs I cannot scream sit up She is asleep. The rain in the darkness I lie in the doorway a figure I want to see and the light is on a sanguinely allcolored demon You are my friend That voice growl stentorian comes from the walls the room You are my friend the fleer her fleer she is asleep you are my friend sardonic grin I jumpsitup in darkness a big house walls room filled up to my neck with the lights are on and nothing then a crawling hundreds bug babies brown black I kick the scurry scatter desperately too many on my legs my legs I you are my friend nothing in the doorway and she fleers and flicks a moment kisses She is asleep you are my friend It's there! my head turns a glimpse You are my friend she says the darkness still outside the rain the axe worshipped as God cancer cuts through the wall into her head her open skull my face pushed in my lips inside she grins rips off my cheek an insect underneath moves past my eye into my nose too big to leave it tries desperately I pull the blood streaming forth she fleers You are my friend upright she looks He's in the window I look bloodless nothing Demons she sleeps Remission What did you what did you say demons What did you what wake what did you up say demons blood in the figure did you in the doorsay wake what did you answer say what did demons say you are up in the window did you say demons my what wake did in up the say what friend did wake you up wake up in the what window demons are in the what did you say wake up my what in the wake did demons in the what

Remission. Reprieve. Wake up.

She Told Me; I Did Not Tell Her

Asya was telling me about her father's death. We were sitting in this beautiful kitchen, this beautiful kitchen in the Bellevue house where she was renting a room. We had not seen each other since before Christmas, when she had gone to Abilene to be with her family. This kitchen was like the ones in those big houses in the movies. It had the big wooden chopping table and the pot rack suspending matching copper cookery, the stainless steel refrigerator, the breakfast nook with white benches below French windows, where I sat shelling peanuts from a basket in front of me, sliding them into my mouth.

Since her arrival he had been in and out of consciousness. On Christmas Eve one of her brothers set up a small tree and a bowl of Jack Daniel's eggnog, and they all just hung out, trying to make the best of it. At one point her father woke up and struggled to stay coherent, calling each one of them over for a private moment. It was the first time he had cried since entering the hospital. She thought he knew this was the last time he would be able to communicate with them.

She spent all night in his room listening to his breathing, counting the breaths, hearing their sound. Eighteen breaths a minute, she told me, that was how it had been all night: eighteen breaths a minute. He had a coughing fit, then she started counting again: twelve. Twelve breaths a minute. After about three minutes, it went back up to eighteen. Then it began to come down, slowly: sixteen, fourteen, twelve, ten. None of her brothers came. It went down to seven. That was her last memory of her father's life: he breathed seven times in his last minute, slowly. In, out. In. Out. Seven times. This will always be the last thing she remembers. He breathed seven times, and then died. No one else came.

Not so long before, my mother had told us about when her father died, how she was the only one there, too. She had talked to him in his unconsciousness, telling him that she loved him, how much she loved him. Finally, she told him it was okay for him to leave them, it was okay for him to die. She said a tear rolled down his cheek, from his left eye, and then he stopped breathing. The last moments of someone's life. I remember when she told us this, in the airport in Kentucky on the journey home from his funeral. I saw my sister (not too far from her own death) start to cry, letting herself fall into my father's arms.

I wanted to tell her all of this, and that her being there mattered, that having someone there makes a difference. I wanted her to feel that her father knew she was there, that he was not alone, that he did not have to die alone, that it mattered. I wanted to tell her this, but I could not, would not. I sat there shelling peanuts, shelling them but not even eating them anymore.

Faith (I'm Afraid It's Not)

Look, I say, arms halfway extended, upturned hands spread open and bouncing up and down, just because I feel something, because I feel it's right, because I believe I know it to be true, it doesn't follow that it must be so. I am brain and body and history—show me something else! I know I can be fooled and can fool myself. I may feel something but that's all I know it is: a feeling. I can't invest in that, that possibility of error, of being attached to phantoms, of my love for you being love, yes, but for nothing except a fabrication of my mind. I was thinking about this the other day and how pessimistic I am, how I shy away as if repelled, turn inward or steer in a direction I don't really want to go, how it's doomed to fail between us, because one way or the other we will part, fucking life, piece of shit, of how our being together doesn't really exist and what that makes me want to do, and you texted me right then saying I was in your mind's eye, I love you, that was all. Just words on a screen and I was crying, the phone still in my hand, crying from the joy of believing that it might be true, crying for both that and its opposite pull: that what I felt might be a response to nothing that's really here.

Room II (the Concurrently-Running Sequel)

It was a circular room, all windows, nowhere to hide. Prime mall real estate, to be sure. There was a sign. *Put yourself here*, it said. *Space available*.

Three of the Happiest Days of Our Lives

iii.   "David Gilmour and Kate Bush" I suggested a week before the party, "It will take some explaining, but," and she was transformed into a 7-year-old on Christmas morning, that smile, those bulging, luminous, voluminous eyes. She had been the one to tell me of their link, and that I put it together, us and them, the age difference just the same. A wig and some makeup, the tights/jacket/heels combo of *Live at Hammersmith Odeon*, she looked pretty close but for the darker skin tone. I was hopeless, but a long wig on my head, a prism sticker on my black Strat, crooning lines from "Hey You" between brags about my little protégé and edifications that "No, I'm the other guy," everyone got the point. She insisted on a performance for the costume contest, explaining how this was one of their collaborations (because setting the right context can make all the difference) while I loaded the CD, then her lip sync, my guitar, goddamn if I didn't hit every note, you couldn't hear it but I knew, I was right there, I remember it like it was now, those last moments: *Don't ever think that you can't change the past and the future / You might not, not think so now / But just you wait and see. . . .*

ii. December 14, 2010, Anaheim, CA. "I never thought I'd live to see it!" she declaimed, breathless, obliviously contributing irony and concinnity.   "We came in," he whisper kissed a snowflake ear, lights down, cue Pink, in the flesh.

i. "Hurry up, Duckie!" she giggled as he fumbled to get Side 2 on the turntable. "It's supposed to flow, you know."

The Amsterdam Gods

You had never looked so vibrant.   "Look, it's beautiful, beauty-full!" You spun in place with your arms outstretched, eyes closed and smiling, water beading on your pretty skin. Everything looked like colors of clay, those browns, those greens, the white and gray, everything toned down by the overcast of the sky. "It's tailor-made for us! Today is tailor-made!" We laughed as we watched you, you always made us laugh. One of us said

"Wait" and snapped a picture of you not waiting. We smiled and looked at each other and said our own little things, not forgetting but not thinking about it, knowing but ignoring, as happy to be there as you, venturing out together up Leidsestraat in a pack, singing your favorite songs: *How I wish, how I wish you were here*. Can you see us? Phil and Cindy Norville, who found each other on a flight to California as they left behind their Texas lives. Abe and Debra Williams, whose son Mitch is named after a dear friend dead ten years now, it seems like it was yesterday, we screamed and ran and laughed. Go and Emily. Ry and Di (Theresa in tow, holding her mother's hand). Jim and Paul Floyd and their wives. Others who shall remain nameless. "The gods are so kind!" you said. I'd have thought you could live forever if I didn't know that by Christmas you'd be gone, probably sooner the doctor had told your father, I'm surprised she's holding up so well.

The Use of Regret

True regret entails living in the present as if you are trying to atone, to make amends, pay tribute to your failures, you can't really make restitution but you do your best, put in the effort anyway, willingly, that's how you want to be now, no regrets, no regrets.

Can Be, Can You

You're outdoors at a café. The weather's nice, you can look at the streetlights changing or the cars going by. But you can refocus, produce your own focus.

Amidst the gentle din, pockets of mechanical music, you discern a brass in the breeze. Look, locate the cause: a man in a minivan with trumpet to mouth. Laugh because you find it pleasant, what called your attention, your attention being called. Make an effort to relinquish your control, or the illusion of your control if that's what it is, close your eyes, it's easier

And hear (what is called *hear*, your experience of hearing, whatever it is) the sympathetic chugs of tuneful rhythm right and left against a backdrop of whirr, don't wed any sound to its immanence, by an act of anoesis forget that it's burnt diesel and experience the slightly pungent pleasant smell as novelty, engineer for yourself novel uses for the same old engines. The harmonies slide upwards, change partners, create themselves anew, gain and lose components, moving left to right (and much more softly right to left), the sound and its cause, the sound and the smell, take them as separate or in contexts as is useful, with or without knowledge, opinion, preference, degree of understanding the process, desire, intent, all aspects, all real things. And the things themselves, the *Ding an sich* outside the *Erlebnis*, the molecules, the air displacement, God if God exists, the dream if I am dreaming, whatever makes it up.

There is this world out there, raging, huge, incomprehensible, some parts desirable but all in all a clumsy violently staggering horror. You want to invite selectively, open the door the smallest smidgen: Welcome, you're welcome, just you. But there is the worry of an unrelated segment forcing its way in, through a far wall, a drunk-drivin' man in a Dodge Caravan, the lightning bolt, the sci-fi sunbeam from space, the despite a life of healthy living, the alley in the middle of the night. Panic for a way to buttress the barrier, panic because you know nothing is impenetrable.

Sometimes you can't help but link the two, can't help but feel that invitations increase the likelihood of party-crashers. But they are not inextricably bound. You can sit at home and all but eliminate winding up under a particular kind of headline (HUSBAND, FATHER KILLED BY DRUNK DRIVER), but you can be gotten to anywhere, you never know, out of the blue and through the roof, had you been at the café you'd be safe. And so you don't stay inside all the time. Because what kind of life is that?

Face

I don't know what you'd think seeing me at the mirror now. I always linger, my eyes hovering about my image: my hairline, my pores and lips, the contours of my jawbone, a nostril, wrinkled skin, the eyes themselves. My expression is always neutral, empty. It seems I am searching for something, I don't know what, the impetus hidden from my consciousness (a euphemism for the fact that I am the one doing the hiding). But I persist, obsessively, knowing all the while that I will find nothing but a face both familiar and utterly alien, a face providing no comfort, no answer, no relief from my inscrutable quest, a face, my face.

The World's Longest, Most Philosophical, Stupidest Greeting Card

A sublimely beautiful thought for the compassionate (and thereby would-be) solipsist is that truly he is the only person in existence. In the atomistic moment when it seems as if the thought might be fact, the thinker is moved by the idea that, although his plight in his phenomenological world is essentially unchanged, the entirety of the suffering he formerly thought to have existed "out there" is not and never was. In that moment, the thinker is overcome with a selfless bliss; and although he cannot help but feel a pang of infinite loneliness from the depth of his isolation (which he now knows to be total), he finds that a small trade-off against losing the suffering of billions over time.

Solipsism, though, is untenable. But this realization is not a product of deduction. As regards that path, the irony of

Meditations cannot be missed: *Cogito ergo sum* is the very foundation of solipsism, because, while solipsism recognizes both the primacy and unassailable nature of this statement (proven true by the thinker's very experience), since nothing else holds such a uniquely axiomatic status, nothing else is accorded the same inherent verity (whereas the rest of *Meditations* suffers fatally from an inability to recognize the unique nature of its own base). No, to set out on any path of deduction beginning with the shining Cartesian moment immediately leads to a dead end. It is something else entirely that lays waste to the solipsistic landscape: the *cogito* of the other. It is true that, as I write these words, the only thing I can independently verify—or verify at all, really—is that I am experiencing. What I am experiencing may be subjective, distorted, even entirely false, but that I am *experiencing* is self-evident. And while I cannot verify there to be another who experiences, the other verifies it for me; and so although I may never be in possession of proof of the other, the proof is nonetheless there. While others might say, "You cannot know whether I am anything more than a figment of your imagination," they indeed bear inescapable witness that this is not the case; and so while their assertion may have rhetorical value, in the end it is nothing more than purposeful sophistry, since they know the falsity of their words even as they utter them. You are my proof, and I am yours.

What appears most likely is that the ontological truth is quite simpler. To examine the situation empirically, one may consider only the available evidence—and what this suggests is that we all exist in a shared physical reality neither emanating from nor giving way to anything transcendent, as inexplicable as this may be (which, of course, is no more inexplicable than were it the case that the transcendent model is the true one). While this is not a gratifying conceptualization, at the same time it is not nearly as bleak as we have been conditioned to view it. The existential implication is that life is a continual present, with no past and future outside this continuum. Thus, a certain kind of solace, even security, may be found along with the philosophically neutral resignation that is a natural complement to this conceptualization, for all one can do then is attempt to attain as much comfort as possible for the duration of the present moment, knowing that no suffering or horror is without an end; and that for the individual there is no price to be paid for the mistakes or failures of a lifetime once that lifetime comes to its conclusion.

[Open. Inside:]

I hope you're feeling better (now)!

[Beneath, handwritten:]

Love, PG-1, PG-2, PG-3 . . .

Bridge View, Part 1

Black glass rippling

Wind-disturbed opacity

A canal at night

Place Names and Places C

John Wayne/Orange County (the "OC") International Airport, SNA (Santa Ana). The Airport can be accessed by the I-405 Freeway, the SR-55 Freeway, and the SR-73 San Joaquin Hills Transportation Corridor Toll Road. Directions to the Terminal: Traveling north from San Diego: Take the I-5 North to the 405 North. Exit MacArthur Blvd. Turn left to Airport Way. The Terminal entrance is on the right. Traveling south from the South Bay: Take the 405 South. Exit MacArthur Blvd. Turn left on MacArthur. The Terminal entrance is straight across MacArthur Blvd. Traveling south from Los Angeles: Take the I-5 South to the 55 South. Take the transition to the 405 South. Stay in the right lane and exit at John Wayne Airport. Traveling from Riverside: Take the 91 West to the 55 South. Take the transition to the 405 South. Stay in the right lane and exit at John Wayne Airport. Directions to Main Street Parking (Off-site Parking): Exit MacArthur Blvd. Turn right (northeast) on MacArthur if coming north from San Diego or south from the South Bay, left (northeast) if coming south from Los Angeles or from Riverside. Turn left (the opposite of southeast) on Main Street if coming north from San Diego or south from the South Bay, right (not southwest, southeast, or northeast, but whatever's left) if coming south from Los Angeles or from Riverside. Main Street Parking lot is on the left after Sky Park. 4 miles from Irvine, 6 from Santa Ana, 8 from Newport Beach, 11 from Orange, 16 from Anaheim, 21 from Brea, 40 from Los Angeles, 472 from San Francisco, 696 from the Wasatch Mountains, 1188 from Sea-Tac, 1364 from St. Louis, 1258 from Abilene, 1410 from the outskirts of Austin, 1410 from a spot near the Texas/Mexico border not too far from Laredo, 1498 from DFW, 1534 from Tyler, 2551 from Honolulu, 2861 from New York City, a world away from Amsterdam.

I Was Thinking of You

I was thinking of you the other night while sitting here looking out across the city grid, my third cat just a kitten ("third" because they always die in the end), asleep and purring on my lap, just a kitten and not the cat she might become ("might" because you never know), purring, vibrating me with her life. It was the first time I'd really remembered you since, replayed scenes with you in them. I remembered that fight we had just after we moved back to Southern C-A, how in frustration at my shutting down you hit the table and that hot soup splashed all over me. It's over and you're gone, and I remembered it and laughed. You're forgiven without my hearing you ask, without your even having to, and maybe I'm forgiven too, forgiven before we can forgive, it's funny, I laughed, forgive me, I laughed.

Ceci n'est pas une pipe

I dropped my pipe the second night in the American Hotel. I was startled as it bounced against the side of the table and then my knee as it fell to the carpet. After a moment of stillness, the tiny echo of adrenaline already dying away all throughout my being, I laughed, forgetting about her for a moment, forgetting about you, and why not?

How They Say It

Dostoyevsky said or one of his characters (it's interesting to consider how much one presumes the other): There's this rock see, and it's, like, a million tons suspended a hundred feet above your head. It'll be going plenty fast by the time it squishes you dead like a bug, mister. You'll die instantaneously, right? says the one. Sure, says the other. No pain? asks the one guy. I rather doubt it, says the two. But would you be afraid there *would* be pain? I would—that's what he says, that's what I say too: I'd fear it, I do. Dostoyevsky conveys this to me and I explain it to you out there or you see it here for the second time or recognize it in yourself, not the words but something.

I was walking through my old neighborhood. (Isn't that how they say it: THE OLD NEIGHBORHOOD?) But it was truly old now. Newly built when we had moved there 30 years before, there was something unchanged, frozen since then. The house-fronts wore the same faces, retained their phrenological features, just a tumor here or there, just a tumor, nothing but a little ol' tumor. The colors though were not the same, shuffled, redistributed I'm guessing, I could not remember exactly the original shades, only that these were brighter stronger gaudier more artificial-seeming. The topography seemed right, the trees and foliage more abundant, older, more mature but of about the same population as then. Shortly after the funeral I moved to live on campus. I hated it, hated the apartments that followed one after the other as I worked my way through the cluster of complexes built with students in mind, I shouldn't have come back. I shouldn't have come back, and 2 years later my father had left with the Rams for St. Louis and I had moved to Seattle for grad school, leaving my mother alone in the house where our pixie left us.

The old neighborhood appears deserted, the wind is blowing,

the air is so clear, the light is beautiful and I'm out for a walk in the perfectly comfortable sharp brisk clear. I'm walking in the direction of the clouds, for some reason all wind-shuttled to a northern distance, clustered far away for my viewing pleasure. The moon is full and big and bright early this evening, luminescent white and pale daytime grayblue occupying the same celestial plane. The old neighborhood has been left to me. The roots of an old tree break through the ground, skim the surface through the grass. The poem carved into the trunk by a teenage me while my sister watched can still be read, surviving juvenilia:

> Another time, another place
> Shoot a death ray into space
> Another place, another time
> Give a little, change your mind
> Another day, another life
> Live it different, how you might
> Another fate, another line
> Move a little, what do you find?

It seems every house has wind chimes and every tree is rustling, there's no traffic anywhere, every car an idle metal shell today, for all I know never-driven props. It's like a diorama approximating the old neighborhood 30 years later, a good job all in all, impressive, a virtual resurrection. I am wondering why but not sure at what, *Why does it exist*, I think that's it, *Why does it exist*, not the cause-and-effect why, the bigger one: *Why?* Why am I shown what I am shown, why do I see what I see, and what is it? At least that something, a feeling, not these words, "why am I at least that not these," not why but something out there. Eventually people filter back in, are let in, a man and his dog, he shortens the lead, bringing it around his wedding-ring hand in loops, a responsible courteous dog-owner in a Raiders cap. The dog is cute, puffy white fur well kempt, of pleasant demeanor, too small to pose a threat. The man smiles, says "How're you doin'?" genuinely, sincerely, seemingly not a miserable man. "I'm fine, thanks" I say since I believe it really was a question, "How are you?" I want to know, especially as there's little doubt he's well, it's almost too far for him to answer over a shoulder, "Good" he says, "Good" I say. A jogger wearing headphones waddles along the street; we acknowledge each other with smiles.

5, she's 5 back in that old neighborhood, where we've moved because of CHOC, our dad having gotten a job with the Rams. I turn left into our hilly housing tract, and just before I make a right that will take me to the top of our cul-de-sac, I catch sight of her on my old Big Wheel as she barrels down the sidewalk. She takes a turn too fast, and the Big Wheel slides off the curb. She's at the top of the steepest hill in the neighborhood, and she has too much momentum to stop herself from starting to slide downwards, as if pulled by the rapids at the top of an asphalt waterfall. I can see her mortal terror, her little feet pushing at the ground without finding a foothold, her little body spasming. I jerked the car out of its turn and accelerated to the mouth of the downhill flow. By the time I stopped and stepped onto the pavement she had made some progress slowing the plastic-wheeled vehicle by sheer futile friction, but she was on the way down, the grade too much for her and her panic. I grabbed the back of the little blue seat. At this angle she was heavier than I had anticipated, and I could only slow her and slide down with her, stepping and shuffling. I knew she would be all right now and that she would have been okay even had she tumbled from the top, probably just a bit bumped and bruised but no worse for wear in the long haul, not even psychologically, just left with a little tale to tell: "Remember when I fell down the hill and scraped my arm and got that big bump on my forehead with the ugly scab? It was 3 weeks before it was completely gone." But at the time she didn't know, she was panicked and afraid not of death, not the words, the concept still a bit obscure but something, a present suffering, an overwhelming anxiety, the terror on her face, her little moans. "It's okay" I said to my tiny little sister, my baby baby baby, "it's okay." "Per-ry" she sobbed and screamed. "It's okay," my footfalls already leveling out, the ground flattening. We stopped, clearly out of danger, even had it been the gravest sort, but she screamed and wailed, I grabbed her from behind, came around her, took her pixie frame in my arms, I said her name, "it's okay," I said her name, her name. She screamed, still in a panic. She knew I was there, knew she was okay, but the fear she couldn't name had not subsided, she screamed, not yet, I said her name, not yet, not yet.

I wonder whether at 6 she remembered, if at 7 she could have recalled this on her last day, "Do you remember the time . . . ?" I envision her answering, but in here she talks like she's my age: "Oh my God! I was so scared, Perry. It was the strangest thing. There was just this terror! Remember how I screamed, the panic? I couldn't shake it even after we'd stopped. So strange to recall it now. It wasn't me." She wasn't 8, so even if she remembered, but I never asked so I don't know, just that it would be different. "Oh yeah" she might have said, "I was so scared I was gonna fall." "Aw, little scaredy" I would say and tickle her. She would have been tired, I think, but they told me it was a good day for her, a good morning, she was just tired. She knew then, the concept no longer obscure, *Tell Perry I love him*. She was swaddled in one of the terry cloth robes I had given her as presents (yellow for her last birthday, completing a rainbow, "I can wear any colour I like!" she had said, paying no mind to having outgrown most of the others), and I would have tickled her and made her giggle, tired but she loved me and she felt I loved her, "felt" because she couldn't know, *No one ever knows or loves another*. I remember the first time I heard that line, "Yes" I said with the wonder of recognition, the *conocer,* "that's right." But she would have felt she knew, and it would have so happened she was right. Did she know anyway that I loved her as she did her best to make me know by proxy that she loved me? There's enough doubt in this overrated world to choke a fucking moose. I'd said "It won't be for long, a semester." "What does that mean" she asked. "You know, like from the start of school to Christmas vacation, except I'm going in July." "After fireworks" she burst out, hopeful animation. "Yes, I wouldn't miss that with you. That's our Ooh-Aah Day. We have to do it every year." She beamed, my parents standing behind me, loving the enthusiasm I could always get from her no matter what kind of day she was having, what treatments she was suffering through. "You'll be back in time for Christmas, though, and my birthday. Is Amsterdam good? Do they have caribou?" "Is caribou like a mouse?" "No!" she laughed, "it's a moooooooose!" "Where did you learn that?" I tickled. "In school" she squawked. "I think it's cold enough for mooses. Mooses? Meese? Meeses?" "Is it cold like where I was born?" That was Boston in January, wherewhen she came two months early on a New Year's trip back East after the Giants ended the 49ers' quest to repeat. "Something like that" I answered. "It's warm here" she said. "You're right: Southern

118 | *(you are here)*

California is pretty warm." "Southern C-A. I like it, but I wish there would be snow. I want it to be all white one day." "Never happen" I said. "I know" she agreed. From her perspective she had more actual cause to know that I loved her than to predict the weather, not being some child climatology prodigy after all—and she happened to be right, so. "You'll miss Halloween, and Thanksgiving too." "I know" I said, "I know." "How I wish you were staying here" she said. "You're going to make me cry, Pix." It may be an inconsistency to allow this nick of name (the stupid things we say), but there, a nice thought, a little snapshot pix, that word, term, endearment, nice thought outside the context, that context, gone yet surveyed regretfully from here/now. "Why" she asked, little big eyes taking me in. "Because I'll miss you. I'm going to Amsterdam because it's a great thing for me to get to do, but I love you, and even though it's great, it doesn't make up for the things I have to give up to do it, like miss Halloween and Thanksgiving or even just seeing you every day, because I love you, little pixie, little goose, my little baby baby sister," poking at her sides with my hands like little beaks, she laughed, you, like that, "I want to be with you all the days. Well, except when you bug me." I tickled her, she laughed, "I'm not a baby and I don't bug you!" "Oh yes you are and yes you do. I should call you babybug!" "I don't, but if you don't watch out I will, just you wait and see!" And maybe when she said *Tell Perry I love him* she felt she knew, being right after all, please, at least that.

The Last Man on Earth

There is a problem with my masturbation. I am consumed in fruitless simulation. Formerly I would manipulate myself (tug, tug) while thinking of what I find arousing (the acts, the images and sounds), and everything would proceed according to plan. But then I went after more. Masturbating as its own end is well and good, but generally speaking it is ersatz: I want connection, interaction. And so at some misguided juncture I started to chase my desideration. My train of thought, my manipulation, my utterance, all were meant to emulate intercourse, the together space inhabited by one and another. Initially I was on occasion rewarded with a fantastic orgasm—this was *closer*, after all. But soon it became problematic. I am the ultimate authority on what stimulates me, but no matter the power of imagination nor the deftness of one's own touch, the unreality wins out. Because of the burden of complete responsibility (for all her words and movements, for each succeeding image, for how she feels beneath, around me), the plot founders. Even my recollections, the mental replay of the once-real, suffer from this defect: they are my recreations, their self-animation totally expended long ago, their death inextricably bound to their birth, completely evanescent. I cannot fend off the awareness of falsity. With a partner, even were one to receive exactly what is preconceptually desired in each moment, it is spontaneous and comes from without; it is self-perpetuating. Onanism cannot supply what it lacks: otherness. But I have fallen into the habit of pursuing otherness there. I am trying to be in body somewhere I am not, somewhere other than here. I pray I can recover that which I have cast aside. (But prayer, I fear, is yet another means of denying my aloneness. A dangerous precedent has been set.)

An Old Dog Anew

I think I'm going to retire.

Why?

I've had enough of history.

But has history had enough of you, professor? Besides, you can take the boy out of history, but you can't take history out of the boy.

Is that so? Anyway, I'm hardly a boy anymore. So old, so much time gone, so late.

All true, Magoo. Nevertheless, here you are. Where are you going to go, and what would you do there?

and now and make something different. There are things I would do again, people I would see, places, experiences I'd live again, but there's so I want to create, or re-create.

Which ones? Which one's pink? Chortle, she says.

That is not only a terrible pun—is that even a pun?—but an awfully dated reference. Do you know how many great bands have come along since them?

Heresy! Pink Floyd is forever! Beg my forgiveness, and make an offering to Roger Waters, David Gilmour, Nick Mason, Nick Wright, Syd Barrett, Alan Parsons, Bob Ezrin, James Guthrie, and the students of the fourthform music class at Islington Green School in the year of our Lord nineteen-hundred and seventy-nine.

Christ, *Dark Side of the Moon* came out the year *I* was born. Do you know how long ago that was?

Fascinating. But we digress. Look, it's not like you've been so terrible, that you've done unforgivable things, like murder or the Holocaust. Murder. Really, the stories you tell. There truly is terrible in this world. You don't know from terrible, *killer*.

Ever hear of Sir Francis Bartlett? You'll say whatever I want.

Whatever you want whatsoever? Snicker. Doodle. Look, Bartlett hat's memory. Me right here is . . . I don't know— something else, though. And don't I come from somewhere, somewhere out there in the great white realm of not-you, caribou?

The people you loved but you didn't quite know.

I'm sorry.

Who are you apologizing to?

To whom. You. Me. Everybody.

Okay. So, can you forgive yourself?

Forgive.

Yes. You're the only one whose experience you live. What good is this "everybody" of whom you speak?

I don't know. I'm trying. I miss you, us. Really.

Um, hello? What am I, invisible? Right here. And look, I forgive you. See? Believe it?

You did, I think. You would have. I know.

All right then. Now, you wanna did would do something with all this regret, meester?

Okay. I will. I will. Just you wait and see.

Bridge View, Part 2

Together we look
I sneak a glance at you, all
too impermanent

Dinner with Him and Her

Her childhood love had been my excuse. They were still

together when we first met, and later I couldn't stand that they remained friends. I didn't think there was anything wrong with it—I just couldn't stand it. When she accepted his offer to put her up in his apartment during a summer trip she took to New York, I took it as proof she was not completely with me, the proof I had always expected, the beginning of the end.

He's in town visiting a few months after my regretful break-up performance, and the three of us are going out to dinner because that's what she wants. "He's always wanted to meet you," she says on the drive up to his parents' house in Hollywood. "You'll like him." I smile as she introduces us, not meaning it. He asks me whether I've read *The Hot Zone*, he's reading it now, he hands it to me. "Communicability," he says before going back upstairs to finish getting ready. "It's amazing what we can catch from one another." Lou Reed is drifting down from the second story ("Romeo Had Juliette"—one of my favorite songs) (© 1989 Sire Records Company. All rights reserved. Unauthorized duplication is a violation of applicable laws.).

At dinner the conversation unwinds freely. He and I speak at length of our admiration for "The Wall". I drop him off, we shake hands. "It was really nice to meet you," I say, meaning it, adding my regrets that we'd not met before, or not adding them, I can't recall. "See, Duckster?" she says, lighting up a state-sanctioned joint, smoky smile floating above cashmere as we roll south down the 101, toward the O.C., home.

In my imaginings now he never thinks of me, would be hard-pressed to recall my existence despite her best efforts to remind him. "No, you remember. Remember when we were at dinner? You were *talking* and talking about that fucking Sartre story. The Wall! Give me a fucking break. Hey, I *know* the Wall, mister!" He never thinks of me because he's happy with his life, his family, maybe he did it better, or just because. But of course I can't know. And I don't know whether I think of him because of being the particular variety of me I have become, or whether no matter where my life had gone I would think that this was yet another link that I had failed to forge.

Seawall

i. I recall weekend treks with my father (Irish-English, had never traveled outside the U.S.) down to the water's edge, watching the boats come and go. Invariably I would focus on someone facing us, a single soul. He or she would be too distant for me to resolve the facial details, and it always haunted me that this other might be looking back just then, engaged in the same process, similarly haunted, no way to tell. We might have tried waving to each other, even sending out a call across the water, but the gesture might always be misunderstood; we could never know what it meant.[2]

ii. February 7, 1980, an all-day drive to Los Angeles, CA, to go to the show, that very first time. So much was eluding me, sunshine, but there was something I understood, even then.

Gravid

They were together watching TV, he with an arm around her shoulders, and at the commercial break he looked her up and down with wonderment. "You're so preggo, hun!"

"I am not," she protested, turning her face away.

"What do you mean? Honey, in case you hadn't noticed, you're as big as a house."

"Jesus!"

"Well, it's just that I'm worried. You seem to have forgotten your condition. I need you to be clear about it—otherwise, you're likely to starting smoking or doing belly flops on the floor."

"I *know* I'm pregnant; I'm just not *that*."

"Preggo?"

"Yes."

---

[2] Lean Larry, the trainer, told an older me he was happiest when on the road for away games. He came to the docks to fantasize about finally sailing away, alone, never to come ashore. He half-succeeded: I'm not sure he was ever really here.

"That's just semantics."

"It's *stupid* is what it is. 'Preggo.' Mr. Ph.D. Professor Asshole."

"But when you're so preggo, you gotta say 'preggo.' And so in your case . . ."

Terry turned back to face him. "How many ways are you going to tell me I'm fucking fat tonight?"

"Honey, you're not fat."

"I'm not fat tonight, you mean, ha ha, very funny."

"You're not fat."

She frowned, then started to sob slightly. "I'm huge!"

"Honey. Aw, c'mere." He gently pulled her shoulders to his chest.

"As big as a house."

"You are not."

She quarter-heartedly shook him off. "You just fucking *said* that."

"Well, yes, I did. I mean, you're pretty preggo, hun."

"You're such a dick. Get off me."

"Oh, honey, come on." He took her hand and stood. "Here, stand up."

"No."

"Come on, stand up."

"What are you doing?"

"Just stand up."

Reluctantly, she began the effort to rise, pushing against the back of the couch with her free hand, which sank awkwardly into a cushion, compromising her efforts. Her loving husband helped her to her feet, then squared up to her.

"Baby," he said, kissing, "you're beautiful, and I love you." He descended to his knees, sliding her shirt up over her convexity.

"What are you doing?" she giggled, resting her hands near her solar plexus.

"You're beautiful, my beautiful missus." He ran his hands over her belly, worshipping, he kissed it, left, right. She laughed, smiled silently, flushed with pleasure. "And this, this is my child," he kissed, "yes," he kissed, "my baby," he kissed, "yes."

Favorite U.S. Pastimes 101 (Early 21st Century)

JERRY RICE (b. 1962), American football player (aka JR, Fifi, the San Francisco Treat, the GOAT). Wide receiver. Drafted no. 1 by the SAN FRANCISCO 49ERS (no. 16 overall) in the 1985 NATIONAL FOOTBALL LEAGUE draft. Retired in 2004 as the NFL's all-time leader in receptions (1,549), receiving yards (22,895), and receiving touchdowns (197). Elected to NATIONAL FOOTBALL LEAGUE HALL OF FAME (first ballot). Wore no. 80

throughout his playing career (including while with the 49ers, who retired the number in his honor), including while with the SEATTLE SEAHAWKS, who had retired no. 80 in honor of STEVE LARGENT (b. 1954), American football player. Wide receiver. Drafted no. 4 by the HOUSTON OILERS (no. 117 overall) in the 1976 NATIONAL FOOTBALL LEAGUE draft. Retired in 1989 as the NFL's all-time leader in receptions (819), receiving yards (13,089), and receiving touchdowns (100). Elected to NATIONAL FOOTBALL LEAGUE HALL OF FAME (first ballot). [more]

Blood Is Thicker

"Aw, Theresa, what's wrong?" Ryan cooed.

Diane gave him an amused smile as she leaned in for a hug "She just started up. Theresa, Theresa," she said, jiggling the six-month-old on the first syllable each time, to no effect on the child's crying. She rolled her eyes in annoyance. "Jesus."

Ryan led them into the living room. "Just the baby today?"

"Yeah. Nelson's at camp this week. Didn't I tell you?"

"Camp?"

"Sports camp over at the university," she called over her shoulder as she went to deposit Theresa in the den. "He's got soccer—sorry: *football*, he's insisting we call it—swimming . . . Something else, too."

"Wow. He must love it."

"Fencing," she said re-emerging from the hallway. "Yeah, he's in heaven."

"He didn't mention it."

"We didn't know until Thursday. Lee told me the wrong deadline, and we were late signing up. But a couple kids canceled last-minute, so Nelson got in."

"That's great. I can't wait to hear all about it."

"Oh, I'm sure you will. Today's only the third day, and I've already heard *plenty*. Well, I gotta get going." They moved towards the front door. "How's Wendy?"

"She's good."

"We've got to get together soon. Tell her to call me."

"Okay. Maybe we can do something some Sunday next month, fire up the barbecue."

"We'll see."

"Lee's good?"

"Yeah. He's gonna be late today. He'll pick her up around 7. She hasn't had a nap, so she should sleep for a while."

"No problemo," he said, pulling the door open. "I'll talk to you soon."

"Okay. Bye."

He took a couple of steps outside and watched her move to

her silver station wagon, black heels click-clacking against the light gray driveway cement. She maneuvered herself into the car. The engine started up. She flipped the maroon sun visor down with one hand, backed the car into the street, waved goodbye almost without looking. He beheld the griseous street, the pulsing azure sky. After a few beats, he stepped back into the house and closed the door. Turning gingerly, he made his way into the hall, then into the first room on the left. He approached the orange crib and observed his niece, fallen into a restless slumber. He reached down and delicately stroked her left temple with the back of his right hand, her fine auburn hair. Her left cheek was warm, rosy, soft. He peeled off the indigo blanket his sister had cuddled around her daughter, revealing stumpy legs. Gently he undid the white diaper, first the right tab, then the left. Theresa stirred. He bent down and kissed her lightly on her hot skin, then stood aright. His erection pained him. He unbuttoned his blue jeans and pulled the waistband of his briefs outward, freeing his phallus. He exhaled from his depths and began to stroke himself, staring at the baby's vagina. He lowered his right hand back into the crib, to the vagina, which now held the entirety of his attention. He touched it with his middle finger. The awakened child began to moan, then to wail. His breathing became more pronounced and rapid, and he inserted the tip of his finger, farther,

farther. Theresa's wails became screams, and her uncle tugged violently on himself, murmuring, "Oh, oh."

What She Might Be Like

What do you think she'll be like, she asks, lying across him, big as a house.

A big mutt, he says.

Charming.

Don't shoot the messenger. Consider the facts: Look at you. Anyone this preggo . . .

She pops him on the chest with the flat of her hand.

And regarding 'mutt': Again I say, Look at you: half-Indian, half-Pakistani, half-Moroccan, half-white. . . .

You just made two of me, mouse to mice. And there's no such thing as white. And what about you?

That's what I'm saying. You're AKC material compared to me, white American mutt, part-everything.

It worked out okay in this case, she says, kissing him on the mouth. You're everything, and it's okay.

What, he asks when her countenance suddenly changes, though he feels the answer before she gives it.

My water just broke, she says, the slightest smile on those lips he just kissed.

Taxicab Horror Stories, No. 80,911

I was about to round the corner, still a good mile from home. A taxicab pulled behind two stopped cars in the right-hand turn lane. I'd been walking for a while, and my feet were sore. I jogged up to the yellow minivan and gave the front window a gentle knock. "Hey, buddy."

He popped open the door. "Hop in," he said, sounding like something was wrong with his palate.

"Buddy, look, two bucks to drop me off at the Target center just over the freeway. You're going that way anyway, right?" I had the bills in my hand, holding them like I was offering a lick of my Popsicle. "It's like a half-mile. You're going that way already."

"I gotta run the meter." A car in front of him had a chance to go. He saw it, began to move.

"Dude, come on, man. Two bucks for nothing. You're going that way anyway. Here. Come on, man. You're going—"

"Alright," he said, leaning over and snatching the bills.

I hopped in. The little door made a plastic thud, very Fisher-Price. "Good," I said.

He moved us forward, and we swung around the corner. We started up the overpass, and I saw that we were bending toward the on-ramp.

"No no. Dude, what—. Not on the freeway. Dude!"

He looked straight ahead, his arms stiff, staying the course.

"Hey, man!" I was practically yelling. "What's going on?"

We merged into the sparse freeway traffic. It was dusk. "Now, you give me three dollars, man."

"What!" I squeaked. "I just gave you two dollars. What are you talking about? Dude, I said *two dollars* to just take me to the fucking Target center—that's what I said! You didn't have to take me. Now, take me back!"

"Ohhhhhhh yeahhhhhh!" It was a yowl of excitement, not a threat, like he was pumping with adrenaline at being about to go over a waterfall. "Whaauuuuuuuu!"

"Fuck, dude!" I shrieked. "Take me back, you freak!"

"Look, gimme three bucks. Three fucking dollars. Everything else is gonna be a lot more hassle than three dollars, man."

"What the fuck, you fucker," I was choking on the words, "I'm gonna fucking call the cops! You're going to go to jail, you stupid ass. What are you doing?"

"Just three bucks, I let you off, that's it. The cops—. Why hassle, man? Is it worth three bucks? I'll get off at the next off-ramp. Look, just give me the three dollars, cut your losses, man. "

"*Cut my losses*, you fuck? I should fucking kill you, you deserve it, but I don't believe in violence. You fuck. But if you touch me I'll fucking *kill* you, I swear to fucking God!"

"Hey, I'm not gonna touch you, man. Jesus, dude! Woo-hoo, man. But just three bucks, come on—the hassle's over. Just come on, just give it to me."

"Goddamn it."

"Just calm down. Just think about it. Three measly dollars."

"Goddamn it goddamn it goddamn it! Okay! Here, [reaching for my wallet] you fuck, you fucking freak, I hate your goddamn guts. Just let me out, you goddamn cunt. You're a terrible person. I should kill you, I should fucking kill you. Here!" I threw three ones at him. "You fucker. You fuck."

We glided down the off-ramp, carefully, gingerly, both of us staring straight ahead. I felt so flushed and stiff I thought I might tighten up and choke to death. He gathered the bills as unobtrusively as possible and pushed them into his shirt pocket. I noticed for the first time that the radio was on (a steadily lumbering Led Zeppelin tune I'd been hearing all my life without knowing its name).

"Hey," he chattered softly, "ever notice how '*e pluribus unum*' isn't on bigger bills? It's only on ones and change—ones and parts of ones . . . 'Cents': a percent of one . . . It's got to be intentional, ya know? They gotta have in mind . . . because, you know, it means 'from many, one,' see? All the *parts* of one say it, and all the *ones* . . . It's all of us: the philosophers, the poets . . . We're all a part. We're ch- . . . ," he swallowed, "-ained. I read about it on Wikipedia. You should check it out."

"Here," I said, pointing to a bus stop, "let me out, asshole."

He eased us to a halt. I opened the door, looking at him warily as I extricated myself, speaking only once I was safely on the curb: "You goddamn fucker. I'm getting your license plate, your information—I'm calling your cab company, the cops. . . ."

"Go fuck a duck!" he called, yanking the door closed. He gunned the engine, and his tires ground gravel angrily.

"That's goddamn fuck . . . Fuck you, fucker, mother. . . ." I was having trouble breathing, my chest heaving with tension that had nowhere to go. Three bucks. The worst thing was that he was right: it wasn't worth it. I knew I wasn't calling anybody. I hadn't even glanced at his license plate.

Remember, Forget

Memory, even more than the verifiable facts, is that which acts as the great signifier of having lived. As intangible, delicate, erring, and often ephemeral as it may be, this faculty defines not only who one has been but also who one is and who others are in relation to the remembering individual. Without memory, there has been no life, the present pulverized into atoms of pure sensoria, unframed, sans meaning.

Intermixed within the memorious storehouse that is my mind are certain dreams. I am not speaking of dreams "memorable" of their own accord, those recurring nightmares and surprising Jungian archetypes, but of others, dreams which are no more noteworthy than the thousands upon thousands of ones long-forgotten. The dreams of which I speak are ordinary, forgettable—save for the single but all-important fact that they *are* remembered. On occasion, when one of these dreams has receded far enough into my past without slipping entirely into the void of the forgotten, it will surface in my consciousness as a memory outside of any context wherein I know it to be a dream. And for a moment I will hesitate: Was that a dream, or did it happen? Usually, with a little effort (or fact-checking in the most extreme cases), I can resolve the question. But a few have proven impervious to my labors, Gordian knots that I cannot untie. I have the sense they may be dreams, but in my perception they seem as real as do other memories documenting a corresponding event or epoch. (And it so happens there are remembered incidents I suspected to be dreams but later came to find actually had transpired.)

As the years go by, I have found myself increasingly in doubt, treading water in an overflowing river of memory questions (questionable memories). But I have learned to accept my Lethean submersion, since in general these remembered dreams I find less discomforting than the mischance and failure comprising the majority of my verifiable life. It is my hope that as I age my memory will be ever more flooded by this phenomenon, so that finally the foundation of the cerebral storehouse of my life is completely undermined. Then will I welcome the remembrances of my life, a life so much more alive and worth recollecting than this sunken flotilla in which I am entombed.

And since in neuronal terms memory is (re)creation, a necessary fiction, nothing real will have been lost.[3] I will drain the polder, and build anew.

After a Lifetime of Healthy Living

She never gets sick, goes through life without so much as a fever or a chill. And then it comes. He finds her naked on the bathroom floor, an arm prone unnaturally against the toilet rim, head lolling on a shoulder, mouth slack, out of control. She's

---

[3] I'm sorry, my baby, I can't just stop. I put this moment here (when we first met, when I found out, the color and the taste, a sobriquet, a smile, a missed chance or mistake), I juxtapose this and that and consider them anew, I take another listen to verses I know by heart, finish to start, because something better might come along, a better way of putting it all together. ("You always have some regrets about losing [someone], don't you?" –DAVID GILMOUR. I'm sorry, my baby, I just can't stop.)

trying to move or stand and she's shitting herself, blood, and he goes to her, she's drooling, and he pulls her off the porcelain, taking her in his arms, supporting her by the back and the base of her skull. He doesn't think of her cellulite, of the dimpling of her thighs against the linoleum, he isn't so unforgivably small, so base. "Oh baby," he says, sparing her the *What's wrong?* that clearly she's in no shape to answer. He lowers her to the floor without thinking about his needs, about being alone, about wanting her to live out of fear that no one else will ever want him. He sees her shitting and blood and isn't the least disgusted, he doesn't smell how bad it smells, he only thinks of her, of not letting her lie in it because that might worsen her suffering, he doesn't know whether it matters to her right now, he's not sure what she's experiencing, just that it doesn't look good. He's worried about her suffering and about moving her, about what he should and shouldn't do, he has no idea. "Baby," he says, "oh baby. Hey, can you hear me? I'm right here."

He doesn't yell, he doesn't think anyone will hear him and he thinks his yelling might increase her stress, the jarring volume, his terror. "Baby," he says, "I love you, I'm right here. Listen, I've got to call 9-1-1, baby. I'm going to get the phone. I'll be right back." He puts her down gently and then darts across the carpet and over the bed, grabs the handset, rolls over the bed and back to her, slides his knees forward and gently gathers up her head, her unnaturally sweaty shoulders. He dials, the phone rings once, twice, he hears a human voice: 9-1-1. What's your emergency?

He doesn't stammer, he speaks clearly, he tells the operator exactly what he's seen (without getting distracted by wondering whether *operator* or *dispatcher* is the better word choice here), the shitting, the blood, naked, the toilet, her mouth. He remembers to say that she is pregnant (in case that matters, he doesn't know), says *is*, not the past tense, not a phraseology that stinks of resignation: *She was pregnant, we were going to have a child together but that is over now.* "Yes, she feels hot. I think she's conscious, but it's hard to tell what she's experiencing." He's already given the address, he thinks they probably know but he makes sure. Paramedics are already on the way, sir, please stay on the line.

He feels increasingly desperate as the moments pass, he stays on the line, she seems about the same, she could be having a seizure, it doesn't seem like it but he's not sure. "Is there anything else I should be doing? Oh, I think I hear them." He drops the phone. "Baby, the paramedics are here. Listen, I'm right here, I'm not going anywhere, and the paramedics are going to come in and help you, and we're going to the hospital. I'm right here." He keeps stroking her head, and finally he lets himself cry as he hears the knocking. It occurs to him that he has not unlocked the door. "Oh honey, I'll be right back with help."

They rush to the bathroom and she's there, he can't bear to see her like this, it physically hurts him, there's no numbness or sense of disconnect from everything that's happening, and now he can't get to her because they're in the way. But they're going right to work, they talk to her, speaking more loudly than he had dared, it doesn't sound harsh, sounds like it might be comforting, he just didn't know what to say. They say her name, they had asked about it while crossing the living room rug, they check her pupils, her pulse, her blood pressure. They talk on a two-way radio, pass along vital signs. They gracefully get her on the stretcher, she seems to worsen, moan, seize, a muted scream, she's seizing. The paramedics reconfigure, say her name, look, inject. She calms, he thinks she might be dying. They rush her out the door, he never realizes that he is naked too, is never self-centered enough to think about grabbing some pants.

And get this: she lives. They both live.

U.S. History 101 (Early 21st Century)

(A classroom at the University of Washington: desks, chairs, lectern, a chalkboard on the front wall. First day of the semester. There are no available seats, and several students are standing along the back wall. PROFESSOR GREGSON has just finished taking roll. Of the 37 names he has called, only "Marcia Chapman" is unaccounted for.)

GREGSON: Does anyone know where Marcia Chapman is?

(No answer. A few students turn their heads expectantly.)

Does anyone know Marcia Chapman?

(Silence.)

(Deadpan) Who is Marcia Chapman?

(General laughter.)

(To the back wall) Okay, one seat at most. Any seniors wanting to add? *(Pause)* Juniors?

(Two hands are raised.)

Okay. You can turn in your add slips after class and hope Marcia Chapman doesn't pop in on Wednesday. As for the rest of you, hey, sorry. Thanks for coming. It was a good instinct: I'm a great teacher.

(Laughter. GREGSON continues as the back wall thins out.)

Okay. This is U.S. History 101, which in my hands has little to do with memorizing dates and names, but with exploring what it's been like for people of all sorts to live in this country at various times. If that's not what you were expecting, what can I tell you? My Ph.D. is in philosophy. I guess things are tough all over.

(Laughter.)

Of course you can't really talk about U.S. history without bringing in certain characters and when they did such and such, but really I'm not all that interested in your knowing who held what title or wrote the Constitution or anything like that. Not that it's bad to know who wrote the Constitution.

(Silence.)

That sounds like a nervous silence.

(Uneasy laughter.)

It's Jefferson. Oh, the youth of America!

(Big laugh by all.)

What we'll be focusing on is living in this country through time. Of course it's important that Thomas Jefferson wrote the Constitution—it wouldn't be exactly the Constitution it is had it not been written by him—but being aware of authorship pales in comparison to knowing what the document means in terms of people's lives. Okay. *(Holding up a sheet of paper)* Everyone's got one of these, right? This is the syllabus, and as you see, we'll have two major exams and two term papers—and that's all as far as assignments go. However, you can also see that attendance and participation make up *30 percent* of your grade. Why so much? Because I think it's somewhat absurd that I have to assign you a letter grade—A,

B, C—since how you perform on tests isn't necessarily a real reflection of what you understand. Can you appreciate my dilemma? If I'm going to evaluate you for the purpose of assigning a label—D, E, F—I have to encounter you some-how, get a glimpse into who you are and where you're at. Otherwise it's just random appellation and statistics—and what kind of life is that?

(Laughter.)

And so . . . Let's see. . . .

(He scans the roll sheet until a name stops him.)

Terry? Where are you?

(A freshman seated in the dead center of the room raises her hand. A moment of silence. Then:)

Hi. Nice to meet you. I'll be your professor for the semester.

(A couple of laughs. None are from TERRY, but she is smiling. He walks to TERRY and makes as if to extend his hand, but doesn't; she (TERRY) smiles more warmly than anyone can smile (TERRY).)

Okay, Terry, what would it mean if . . .

The Travel

I am a traveler. I am not well traveled, am not a world traveler, know very little about traveling at all. But I am a traveler now, at this moment. I am in a country other than my own, a place that belongs to someone else, a people other than myself. I am passing through on my way to nowhere (except, eventually, back to the place from whence I came). Although I am not here alone, I seek not company (though neither do I seek to avoid it) but the experience of the traveling, not in the sense of movement but of slowly progressing tortuously (whether randomly or no), traveling, experiencing, simply being in this place, not to say "I was here" but to be here now, to be taken along by the travel, which seems to progress almost on its own. Tomorrow I will be on a plane, the travel ended (except for my conveyance home), but tonight I am a traveler, enjoying greedily and slightly frantically the last moments of the travel, appreciating them as completely as I am able before they are no more, before I go back and witness others passing through the place I live, traveling, sitting in my favorite café and writing about those last moments of their travel before checking out of the hotel, riding in a taxicab to the airport, and boarding Flight 302, departing 4:35 p.m., Gate G, rows 21 through 34 first, we thank you for your patience, come back and see us again.

The Very First

I was staying the night in the old neighborhood, talking with my mother, who

> —persisted in smoking while pregnant with me,
>
> —stopped breast-feeding me at three months,
>
> —stuffed me with empty calories,
>
> —routinely hugged her physical and emotional bulk against me long after the embrace became unwelcome,
>
> —occasionally revoked Christmas and birthday gifts,
>
> —by example infected me with the wily ways of *mauvaise foi*,
>
> —frequently interrupted me with "Stop before you say something you'll regret" (which I took both too literally and not literally enough),
>
> —passed along the gene that killed her,
>
> —said, "Go,"
>
> —said, "Perry, I've got bad news."

"I don't feel old," she said. "I don't feel any different than I did when I was in my forties, or even my thirties. I look different. Sometimes that can affect how you feel about yourself."

She was harmless to me now, this other, she held no sway, this woman I had internalized, this woman whose influence had contributed to my letting rupture every intimacy I had come to meet (something she would never have wished to happen). I looked at her face: it went silver, rufous, aquamarine. I kissed her and watched her as she waddled up to bed. I took a midnight stroll through the empty streets and came to a row of hedges where a steady, three-part soundpulse was washing left to right, left to right: innumerable crickets keeping time in some sort of regulatory miracle, left to right, letting each other know that all was well, that not a one knew of any cause for distress, not right then, not just then.

Blindness, Close

A quasi-illegible letter found with the decedent (identity unknown, addressee unknown):

I am almost blind now. Everything has been reduced to some vague shadows out there, impressions of light and dark, an occasional shape, something I can almost guess. I make the marks by habit, from a memory that's only semi-automatic now, my hand moves to make the strings of symbols, utterance meant to represent my utterance. I write not knowing whether this will reach you, or if it does whether you will be able to make it out. I could have someone read it back to me, voicing the marks, I am almost blind, is that how it started, is that really what I said or what I really meant to say, the doubt, even if it were, even did it get to you without my seeing, even if you responded.

I notice things. I move my arm and my shoulder pops loudly

inside of me, old, pops so hard it moves, there is no pain except that now I think about the feeling I would have preparing for the pop were the process to happen in reverse, the trepidation even while knowing that nothing is wrong, the air puff from the glaucoma machine, I remember, the dread, the feeling of it, in the coming dark I feel it, the fear.

I think it's best that you don't respond, better, all things considered, your writing or coming to my room, hi it's me, I wouldn't trust it, I'm going blind.

I try to picture a duck blind, what is a duck blind, I remember, hiding the meaning, duck blind, poor duck, he's blind or I'm hiding, he can't see me either way. I feel the dread, I know the pop is coming, loud and so hard it moves my shoulder, and the trepidation, the waiting, waiting.

What could you say, it's better you don't respond, best, I don't see you either way. Now I make the marks without dreading whether they will be read, can be read, almost blind now, I am, semi-automatic now, my hand moves, I am

20 Most Popular First Names (US)

Rank	Name (also called)	No.
20.	Paul (Pauly, Paulie, dick (sometimes))	1,348,500
19.	Jennifer (Jenny, Jennie, Jenni, Jeni, Jen(n))	1,360,445
18.	Elizabeth (Liz, Liza, Eliza, Beth)	1,370,170
17.	Daniel (Danny, Dannie, Dan)	1,395,280

16.	Barbara (Barb, Barbar, Babs)	1,435,050
15.	Christopher (Chris, Toph (rare); not Cris)	1,485,125
14.	Linda (Lindy, Linds, Lin, Lin Lin; not Lynn)	1,515,250
13.	Patricia (Patty, Patti, Pat)	1,571,800
12.	Thomas (Tom, Tommy, Tommie, Thom)	2,001,000
11.	Joseph (Joe, Joey, Joel; not Jo, not JoJo)	2,015,500
10.	Charles (Charlie, Charly, Charley, Chuck, Chuckie, Chas)	2,186,600
9.	Richard (Richie, Rich, Ric, Rick, Dick)	2,444,700
8.	David (Dave, Davey, Davie, Davy)	3,391,550
7.	William (Will, Willy, Willie, Bill, Billy, Billie (few))	3,519,150
6.	Michael (Mike, Mikey, Mick (few), Mickster (almost none))	3,774,350
5.	Mary (Mari, Mare, Mother, other)	3,849,750
	Note: Not all females called "Mary" *are named Mary (e.g., Maryanne).*	
4.	Robert (A-hole (sometimes), Robbie, Robby, Rob, Bob, Bobby; not Bobbie)	4,512,400
3.	John (Johnny, Johnnie, Jack (occasionally, for some reason))	4,695,100
2.	James (Jim, Jimmy, Jimmie, boopieboopboop (extremely rare))	4,760,350
1.	I (me)	circa 300,000,000

Honorable mention:
you (you, et al.)   circa 300,000,000 - 1

Lament for an Unpredictable Coat

I returned from the old neighborhood, from my mother, took off my coat (bought during my second stay in Amsterdam) and tossed it on the chair. For the first time I noticed a small blue tag, rectangular, sewn into the lining: six yellow letters, each inside a circle. I started to lean forward to read them, then stopped, closed my eyes, exhaled, relented, relaxed back into the couch, realizing I didn't care what the tag said. Presumably it was nothing more than the brand name or style, information of no consequence.

I wished the world were such that the six letters were a secret message, heretofore hidden but now revealed to me for the undertaking of a grand adventure. In a more spontaneous, more beautiful existence they might spell out ontological truths— ALIENS or GODYES—or simply change every twenty-four hours, imparting a random gift of knowledge pertinent to the day. I would wake up and check tag, gleaning that morning's declaration: MURDER, NORAIN, FORGIV.

It's Strange to Try

It's strange to try to reconcile what you are with what you were if you're someone who feels unequivocally unchanged. Then there is nothing to reconcile; it is all one: you are were now then. But I think about the me then and grimace because supposedly that's me, though I feel like he, a bastard me, is a character in a virtual life, a computer program or game, a simulation I watched unfold. I was there, it was my pinprick of view, but that's not me, I wouldn't do that now, I wouldn't feel that. It's all as if I had been a little over my left shoulder, looking on, as if I could see me from the outside, as if what I experienced was a television series I once watched starring me, that character, not I (me) because I am (he is) here, the I here who remembers watching, I replay the episode in my mind, recollect as well as I am able, and in show of memory it is not me because I don't feel like that, I wasn't there, not me, this here now me, the real one, the one it seems will be me my here forever now, and maybe finally it will, finally, finally.

I Can Only Paraphrase

By this point she was having difficulty talking for any length of time, and it seemed like she saw this as her last opportunity to communicate coherently (which it was). I can only paraphrase:

If you remember me, she said to all of us (parents, brother, childhood love, the Amsterdam Gods), don't remember this, the end, or remember it, but only as part of the whole thing, part of the whole process, the cycle, the flow. Remember that I believe in reincarnation and that I'd do it again, I'd choose to come back even if only to do this all again in just this way with just this ending, this ending that's not ending. Oh, I don't know, she said and laughed a little. I admit it, I'm guilty, I'm petty, I want your sadness, I want for you to miss me, I want you to think of me every time you hear Kate Bush and Pink Floyd and remember how much better my taste in music was than yours, she laughed, and we laughed, but think of me only a little, a little part of all of this and all of you, put me in my place, don't let me crowd anything out, no matter how small or mundane you think it is, not even just a couple of laughs. Remember that you're not alone. Oh, that's not quite right. I know we're alone, I do. What is it? No one ever knows, she said, and I heard the ellipsis of her thoughts, and was thankful she didn't look at me, that she declined to take the victory she could so easily have had, thankful she allowed me to remain intact, regretful but intact, preserved. I know it's true, she said, that no one can ever know what it's like to be you, not really, not at all. Only you can feel the stain of your own existence, my Terryness, the taste of my own mouth, they could never know that, but sometimes his experience isn't so different, I think, she feels somewhat like you feel, there can be this commonality, something that could be truly recognized if only we could see first-hand. It's terrible and beautiful, isn't it, to know that's out there but that it's *out there*? She looked about to cry but didn't, and she chortled once and snorted and wiped her nose and sniffed, and there was viscous mucous on her hand, and I felt guilty that I noticed and that I felt disgust, and I thought: I'm about to lose this person, I'm about to lose her. Laugh more than you're sad, she said, don't forget to laugh, laugh at the sadness, cry and laugh, fucking life, piece of shit, she laughed, laugh in the midst of all of this pain because it doesn't hurt anything and I'm both: the horror and the humor. Look at me, recognize everything, the true, the false, it's all one thing, all together, take in what you can, knowing that you never know, that the story you have is just a story. I'm all of it, and I'll come back and do it all again, I will, I will, just you wait and see.

Another Time, Another Place

She lay on her bed, her body locked and motionless in a state of dreaming, sketchpad of skyscape resting on her chest. She dreamt she was physically ubiquitous, everywhere at once, in all space-time, all dimension. She was awakened at 4:00 a.m. by a whispered impellation: *Water.* She showered sleepily, and when she returned to bed she did so in the dark, for she had neglected to turn on the bedside lamp. As she lay herself down she jumped in alarm at a circle of intense warmth against the center of her back. She switched on the light and saw a hole six inches in circumference burnt cleanly through her mattress and into the floor below. White dust and debris suffused her bed sheet, and in the ceiling above was an opening of a corresponding size, formed by the last remnant of a desperate star, its life force concentrated as a ray across the heavens, its reach belying the fact that it had ceased to exist so many years ago.

Animals Killed by Airplane Refuse

BREA—Several animals were killed and at least three stores were destroyed Monday night as refuse discarded by a passing airliner crashed through the ceiling of the Brea Mall.

The refuse, commonly referred to as "blue ice," was mistakenly jettisoned by an off-course Boeing 767-222, said officials at John Wayne International Airport (SNA), where the inbound United Airlines flight from Hawaii eventually landed.

While several stores suffered some damage, it was Chien et Chat, a pet store, which was hit most severely. Aside from the complete destruction of the store, at least 43 animals were killed, with several others missing and unaccounted for. Pixel Pixie, a digital photography outlet, and Quiet As a..., a store specializing in sleep aids, were also hit hard, their inventories utterly lost.

All three stores were on the mall's upper floor. No stores on the ground floor were damaged, and the damage to other stores on the top level was minimal, according to Brea police.

Officials at SNA declined to speculate as to why the United flight was off of its regular flight plan or why the refuse, which usually would have been jettisoned over the open ocean, was discarded so far inland. An investigation is pending.

Among the animals killed were 80 rare insects, 27 genetically altered mice, 11 psittacines (one that might have appreciated for

$9,000 when fully mature, according to a Chien et Chat employee who wished to remain anonymous), eight snakes, seven monkeys, a number of water fowl, a dog, a cat.

People and Places as Words

She was a little sweaty. It was summer in Southern California (where we moved after she graduated—a homecoming for both of us), but it's always better not to use the air-conditioning if you can help it. The balcony door was open. Emily was in Gina and Opal's apartment across the courtyard (*Go*, we all called them, *Go*). They had been singing along all afternoon, jumping around in time: The Flaming Lips as Pink Floyd, Modest Mouse recalling Pixies, the Pixies doing David Lynch. Now it was David Bowie, playing both narrator and character: *Five years— that's all we got.*

"You'll miss me when I'm gone," Terry said, having exactly 40.0% less time than that.

"Probably."

"Probably?" she squawked, poking at my sides with her hands like little beaks. "*Probably?*"

"Well, baby, something better always might come along."

"Probably," she nodded, her inflection pointing to: *No way, buddy.* "We—*some* of us, anyway—always think that somewhere down the road there's something better, or at least less worse. But you got-ta know when to hold 'em."

"That's a mixed metaphor. Plus bad grammar. And 'The Gambler', for some reason. What fucking year were you born?"

Terry laughed and whirled away. "I like you sometimes, Duckboy," she said, retreating into the hall.

"Yellow-belly. Mouse-livered girl. Afraid to stay and fight. *Ev'ryone considered her the coward OF the coun-ty.*"

"See?" she called, voice barely audible now. "You're missing me already."

Mailboxes, Et Cetera

I remember going with my parents to shop for a mailbox. I was very small, mailbox-level at the mailbox store. So many different types of mailbox, so many different designs. I knew few words to describe them (*mailbox*, some colors, *metal* presumably), I just looked, so many different mailboxes, which one will we get, the variety impressing me somehow. Now I don't care, they're mailboxes, I don't care, I don't appreciate

"Grrr" she says.

I am that child, older, in my own house with its own mailbox, the colors of which I cannot bring to mind without going outside and looking. It performs its intended function; that is all I recall.

But the nexus of thought bring details to mind: the red flag, the loose hinge, the angle of the little roof

"Woof" she says.

"Synonymous with 'weft,' I'm sure" I say.

"Woof woof!" she says.

It's one thing to know about this town, this nation, this earth and dust, how it works, to be familiar with it or be able to explain it, but to live it, to experience it

"Flicker" she says.

It gets generalized, codified, X = happiness or love or fightin' words or what you're supposed to do/be/believe

"Do-be-do-be-do" she says.

There is so much detail, you can get bogged down or caught up, it gets glossed over, flattened into a background mostly of our own making, each of us making our own

"Pshaw" she says.

In the park nearby the natural sounds are compromised by the freeway running north/south in the distance, a phenomenon generally regarded as spoilage and not that amazing constant gentle omnidirectional thrush that Shakespeare could never have imagined

"Shhhh" she says.

I sip this coffee, it's warm, the cream and sugar are just right, it's what I want, it's what I want right now, I have it, here it is, it's worth more to my present moment than the last time we made love, which was incredible, I remember, it was only yesterday, the way your skin was against my lips, you letting me have you, wanting me to have you, that pull inside, the way you looked, the look on your face, your sound, your feel, your hands on me, they moved on me, the way we felt together. The memory is a nice thought, but I sip this coffee now, I have it in my mouth, I swallow, I take this bit of cake, I chew, the cake flattens pliably, smooth chocolate on my tongue, I feel it, it's an ecstasy, it's here right now, it's only cake and coffee, worth so much less than love, but

"Sigh" she says.

Look at you, this poorly-sealed moving meat, holes everywhere, absurd holes, you breathe, in comes air, in and out, vents for gas, a slit for procreation, a hole for piss, a hole for shit, a hole for chewy chocolate cake, some for sound in the sides of your head, dirt can get in, insects, disease, worse

"Glow" she says.

"Are you gonna to do that all night?"

"Every single fucking time I feel like it."

It's bad, it's a bad deal, the present being so dominant, so easy for it to go bad, to stay bad. Having fucked you is nothing if I'm on the rack, your love doesn't dull the pain, not even for a second, those nociceptors just keep firing like we never even met

"Shrug" she says.

"Surely you're going to run out of ideas any time now."

"Don't call me Shirley."

"It's not that I mind. I just don't want you to overtax that cute little brain of yours."

"Nod" she says.

"Wink" I say.

"Nudge" she says, smiling the sly little smile she had.

When it's good, it can be good. But it doesn't cancel out, it doesn't justify, it's not as necessary to have as its opposite to avoid, it'll never last; the other's inescapable, common, behind everything

"Tug" she says.

It's a battle or two, here and there, now and then, once in a while. The war is over, doomed from the start, we lose, victory cannot be had, we're outgunned, outmanned, overwhelmed, over-run, conquered, lost

"Aahooh" she says.

Even if you live forever, and who'd want that, I wouldn't wish that on you, but you won't, we can't stay like this, such a delicate balance, so much weight to tip the scales, so much gravity, gravitation, grave, so grave

"Uh" she says.

"Uh" I say right back.

I Should Have Written

Like that. I should have lived a different story, or lived the same story differently. I should have better told you, should have said: I have seen you, seen you and loved you because of what I have seen. I should not have worried about being silly or morbid or melodramatic, presumptuous, embarrassed, misunderstood. I should have told it to you plainly, in words without art, words I have and can never have, my own words, simple, failing you and failing me, I should have failed and kept on failing.

Sleep Baby Sleep

It's all rods and cones baby, a rods and cones baby, lying here outside and in between us, and it's more rods than cones baby, these grayed colors and shadows, and where you don't see a thing there's almost no light at all, the patches of darkness, the parts out of sight, it's later than late baby, why aren't you sleeping, are you afraid of the things that you see and don't know, don't you know how to pretend, to believe you understand what you see, or are you happy for now in the relative cool, the comfortable gloom, the lack of knowing you're painless, painless for the moment, our nociceptors baby, they're not receiving, lucky you, lucky me, lucky baby all three, but baby it's rods, and that baby means darkness, and that's sleepy time baby, beddy-byes for my babies looking at one another, rods and cones babies, close your eyes close your eyes

√-1

Let us discuss pain.

In discussing pain, let us confine our considerations to the animal kingdom, wherein the validity of DOUBTS about the phenomenon under discussion becomes vanishingly small as through evolutionary time we encounter ever more complex animal BRAINS, with their hundreds of millions of NEURONS, which together create the totality of experience without ever really touching.

Pain has an evolutionary purpose: it stimulates the animal to attempt to avoid causes of pain. Since that which causes pain overwhelmingly tends to be detrimental to the functioning and even existence of the animal, AVOIDANCE of causes of pain enhances the chances of the animal's ability to procreate, thus enhancing the propagation of the species.

Even if the human brain is not capable of generating a greater degree and variety of physical pain than occurs elsewhere in THE ANIMAL KINGDOM (though based on current neurological theory it is not unreasonable to conjecture that some fish do not experience pain, though a dolphin would, a whale, a chimpanzee, not a bug I'm sure, but a cat, a dog), THE HUMAN MIND, quite adept at diverting its apparently singular creativity to the experience of fear, fixation, guilt, etc., probably tips the scales in such a way that we are not off base in supposing that humans are capable of experiencing the greatest suffering in THE KNOWN UNIVERSE.

That capability outstrips the evolutionary efficaciousness of pain. Nature, though, seems to concede this, albeit usually only in extremis. It does so in the form of endogenous opioids, "natural anesthetics" the brain administers to itself to ameliorate the experience of pain.

It would generally be said that endogenous opioids exist to provide a preservative function, temporarily blocking the experience of pain resulting from physical damage so that the animal may be better able to flee the cause of said damage, thus minimizing said cause as an existential threat.

From this conjecture we might reasonably infer a general rule: The greater the damage, the greater the pain; correspondingly, the greater the release of endogenous opioids.

A truism: For an animal, death is the greatest possible state of damage.

A conjecture that is not quite a theory but I know to be true, surely, I know it: at the moment of death all of your opioids are released, a lifetime's worth, no reason to waste them, they are released just as you are, a lifetime's worth of pleasure, overflowing in a single moment, no reason to waste it, and everything goes white, which is to say all colors, overcoming, surrender, you lose yourself on the page, without a word

$\sqrt{-1}$ *Minus One*

I was the one. We had made arrangements, everyone involved compassionate enough to respect that it was over, why should there be any more suffering?

I was the one who injected the morphine, beautiful exogenous opioid, aided by good souls whose names I will take with me to my own grave, giving just the right amount.

I looked down at her, I touched her forehead then jerked my hand away, not wanting to risk disturbing her sleep just because I yearned to be as close to her as I could, have that bond of touch, feel her breathe, for the last times.

She opened her eyes. You opened your eyes. Terry, you opened your eyes. "I love you" I said. "Terry, I love you." I extended a hand, we touched, *Terry*, we touched. "What" I asked, thinking you had said something, just barely, Terry. I looked at you, and somehow you were laughing, quietly but a lifetime's worth of joy, and I felt forgiven, for a moment, for the first time, and I was in love, and it is still love now, it was right now, *this is right now right now* and you were here, right here.

**

Isn't This Where

Now here you are, and we are here, together now and right. There is so little I can give you, regretfully little and late. I can say I love you, I can reach out a hand, I can tell you a story about us and them, paint it any colour you like; I can make these voices sing together, bring all these tones in tune. But all I create becomes broken apart, because what they did on *The Dark Side of the Moon*, that's pretty fucking tough, especially considering originally it was two separate sides and now you can run it through on CD, and fuck, it's perfect, perfect and preserved. Put it together, that's me, so clever, such a character, and anyone can see there's no making amends and no reconciling, not me to you, not me to me, and nothing to be done but this. And yes I know that no one ever knows or loves another, but let me tell you, let me tell you, try, we can try.

Acknowledgments

Several sections of this novel were published previously (generally in earlier forms). Below is an attempt at a complete list:

"I Dream of Bicycles" has appeared in *poeticdiversity*.

Part of "A Weekend, Early" has appeared in *Happy*, *Total Obscurity Magazine*, *Lexicon*, *The Crunge*, and *Bomb Threat* (as "Sunday Afternoon").

"Color Me World" has appeared in *Spot Literary Magazine*.

"In a Bakery" has appeared in *Satori Visions* and *Lexicon*; and in *Bathtub Gin* as part of "The Airliner Triptych, with Seven Motifs".

"Out" has appeared in *Verdad* and *the2ndhand*.

"Another City of Light (On the Wane)" has appeared in *Spot Literary Magazine* (as "Another City of Light").

"In Orange, a City of the Modern Age" has appeared in *The Great American Poetry Show* (as "Anaheim, 2003").

"Undermusic" has appeared in *Pif*, *The Mainline*, and *Bathtub Gin*.

"Forever" has appeared in *Faster Than Sheep* and *Maverick Press*.

"Bliss (Once During Lovemaking)" has appeared in *Aura* (as "Bliss").

"Ephemera" has appeared in *American Jones Building & Maintenance*.

"It Turned Out that Reality Was Overrated" has appeared in *Spot Literary Magazine*; and in *the muse apprentice guild* (as "It Turns Out that Reality Is Overrated").

"Can't Help But See" has appeared in *Trillium Literary Journal*.

"Teeth and Other Things" has appeared in *Lynx Eye* and *As-Is Fiction*.

"A Few Remains" has appeared in *Spot Literary Magazine*.

"Husband, Father Killed by Drunk Driver" has appeared in *poeticdiversity* (as "Ride").

"Taxicab Horror Stories, No. 80,911" has appeared in *the2ndhand* (as "Taxicab Horror Stories, #351") and its 10th-anniversary compilation *All Hands On*.

"Remission" has appeared in *Total Obscurity Magazine*.

"Remember, Forget" has appeared in *the fossil record*.

"Blindness, Close" has appeared in *poeticdiversity*.

"After a Lifetime of Healthy Living" has appeared in *The Interrobang*.

"Lament for an Unpredictable Coat" has appeared in *wigleaf* and *Unknown Writer*.

"Another Time, Another Place" has appeared in *Winedark Sea*, *As-Is Fiction*, and *Satori Visions*.

"Animals Killed by Airplane Refuse" has appeared in *Bathtub Gin* as part of "The Airliner Triptych, with Seven Motifs".

"People and Places as Words" has appeared in *The Dos Passos Review*.

"Mailboxes, Et Cetera" has appeared in *Literary Chaos Magazine* and *The Interrobang*.

+

Additionally:

"In King County, Washington" is an excerpted version of the plea agreement of Gary Ridgway (a.k.a. the Green River Killer).

"Embellishment" is a poem by Todd Balazic (with a title embellished by me), © Todd Balazic. Used by permission. It appeared in my one-off *Rencounter*.

"Jack Valenti Is Near Death (One of Our Jokes) ®" features excerpts from the Motion Picture Association of America's ratings system.

Little bits from 24 songs (plus a paraphrase and three blind mice) appear in this work (call it Fair enough Use):

- ••Lynn Ahrens's "The Preamble" (by Thomas Jefferson, public domain) and a paraphrase of her "A Noun is a Person, Place, or Thing" (© Schoolhouse Rock!)

- ••David Lynch and Alan R. Splet's "In Heaven (Lady in the Radiator Song)" (© David Lynch Music Company)

- ••The Pixies' "I've Been Tired", "Hey", "Caribou" (by Black Francis, © Rice 'n' Beans Music), and "Bam Thwok" (by Kim Deal, © Bug Music)

•• Kate Bush's "The Big Sky", "Jig of Life", and "Love and Anger" (© Kate Bush Music Ltd.)

•• Taj Mahal's "Farther on Down the Road (You Will Accompany Me)" (by Taj Mahal and Jesse Davis, © EMI Music Publishing)

•• The Cure's "How Beautiful You Are" (by Robert Smith, © APB Music Co., Ltd.)

•• David Bowie's "Changes" (© EMI Music Publishing Limited, Tintoretto Music, and Moth Music), "Ashes to Ashes" (© Tintoretto Music/RZO Music Limited (84%) and EMI Music Publishing Limited (16%)) and "Five Years" (© Tintoretto Music/RZO Music Limited (37.5%), EMI Music Publishing Limited (37.5%), and Chrysalis Music Limited (25%))

•• Lou Reed's "Romeo Had Juliette" (© Metal Machine Music)

•• Modest Mouse's "One Chance", "Workin' on Leavin' the Livin'", and "People as Places as People" (by Isaac Brock, © Ugly Casanova)

•• Kenny Rogers's "The Gambler" and "Coward of the County" (by Don Schlitz and by Roger Bowling and Billy Ed Wheeler, respectively, © EMI Music Publishing/Sony ATV Music Publishing LLC and Careers-BMG Music Publishing Inc./MCA Music Publishing, respectively (whew!))

•• Pink Floyd's "Have a Cigar", "Wish You Were Here", and "In the Flesh" (by Roger Waters). Also employed is the spoken line bookending the album *The Wall* (all © Roger Waters Overseas Music Limited/Pink Floyd Music Publishing Ltd.).

For more shea M gauer, who designed the fab cover, check out ontheroughseesofmyeyes.blogspot.com (art).

For more Greggory Moore,
who helped &c.,
visit greggorymoore.com.

Made in the USA
Columbia, SC
11 August 2018